PRAISE FOR
SALLY SLICK AND THE STEEL SYNDICATE

"Sally has a sparky attitude, a mechanical mind, a passel of brothers, and a racing tractor—what more could any good heroine want? You'll want to pick up this ruralpunk adventure story because Miss Sally Slick is the real deal!"

— Dawn Metcalf, author of INDELIBLE

"Sally Slick is a pulp hero for all ages! Whether she's hauling her brothers out of trouble, cracking-wise with gangsters or fighting alongside kung-fu masters, Sally never fails to deliver adventure. Carrie Harris has crafted a story full of heart, intrigue and a healthy heaping of two-fisted justice!"

— Matthew Cody, author of
POWERLESS and WILL IN SCARLET

An Evil Hat Productions Publication
www.evilhat.com • feedback@evilhat.com

First published in 2013 by Evil Hat Productions

Editor: Amanda Valentine
Art: Dani Kaulakis • Design: Fred Hicks
Branding: Chris Hanrahan

Softcover ISBN: 978-1-61317-063-2
Kindle ISBN: 978-1-61317-073-1
ePub ISBN: 978-1-61317-074-8

Printed in the USA

SALLY SLICK
AND THE STEEL SYNDICATE

A TALE OF THE

BY CARRIE HARRIS

CHAPTER 1

The racing tractor's name—Calamity—arched over its body in perfect yellow letters. Sally Slick stepped back to get the full effect, a dripping paintbrush clutched in one hand. She frowned and tilted her head this way and that, trying furiously to figure out what was missing. After all the time she'd put in building the tractor, everything needed to be perfect for Calamity's maiden voyage. Too bad the paint job wouldn't cooperate. The whole thing was so frustrating that Sally kicked over the metal bucket holding her precious tools. They spread across the dirt floor of her workshop with a clatter.

"You okay?"

A timid voice came from the back of the old crib barn Sally had taken over after Pa moved all the livestock over near the east field. Someone must have entered the rarely used door tucked behind towers of wooden crates. She whirled around, brushing at her eye. A dust mote must have gotten into it, because it was all watery. If one of her brothers found her weeping like a mush, they'd never let her live it down. Thankfully, it was just Jet.

Her neighbor and oldest friend stepped into the light, showing his teeth in an uncertain grin. His hair stuck out in about twenty-seven different directions simultaneously, and his wrists extended a few inches too far from the sleeves of his hand-me-down shirt. But he was still a couple of inches shorter than Sally, gangly in a way that suggested his arms and legs might be growing faster than the rest of him and he hadn't quite figured out how to handle that.

"Hey, Jet." Sally turned back to the tractor and sighed.

He edged a little farther into the room, eyeing the corners with the kind of reflexive caution developed by the kids at the bottom of the food chain. "Is it safe?" he asked.

She huffed despite herself. Did he think she was going to leap up and bite his head off?

"Are you afraid of random cutthroats or me?" she asked archly. "Of course it's safe, silly. Come over here. I need your opinion; I'm thinking this doesn't look scary enough."

He stepped up beside her, took one look at the inscription, and whooped. "Wait a minute. Her name's Calamity?! That is the coolest thing. Remember that time we played that adventure where Jet Blackwood and Calamity Sue got captured by the natives on an Egyptian dig, and Blackwood had to pick the locks of their shackles with the bones of pharaohs, and—"

"Of course I remember, goof. I was there. That was a good one."

Not that she'd admit it to anyone but Jet. It was one thing to read adventure tales. A lot of people did, and some of the kids at school swore the stories were true. She wasn't so sure herself, but she knew that the Adventures of Jet Blackwood and Calamity Sue was a kids' game. They'd started playing the made-up adventures when they were eight, and it had been okay back then. But now they were fourteen. That was too old to be climbing up trees and pretending they were rope ladders into an ancient civilization, solving mind-bending puzzles left by the ancients, and beating imaginary bad guys into desperate submission.

They were misfits, all right. He thought he was an action hero, and she didn't fit in with any of the other girls at school—they were all into talking about boys and staring at boys and—if they were particularly daring—kissing boys. Sally had six—no, seven, if you counted the baby—brothers. She'd had enough of boys, thank you very much.

In short, she didn't fit in very well with the girls, and she was careful to keep her head down. Naming the tractor after her character was okay, especially since no one knew about the connection. But Jet took things much further than that, and he got picked on for it. He couldn't stop pretending to be an adventure hero, even going so far as to insist that everyone call him by his "hero" name. Although Sally had to admit that if she had a bum first name like Jackson, she might stick with an alias too. She'd been lucky name-wise—her great-grandparents changed their last name to Slick because no one could pronounce Slusarczyk. So she could understand the reasoning. She just didn't have to like it.

Jet responded the same way he always did when she gave him a hard time, shaking it off and continuing on like nothing had happened. "Yeah, it is missing something, isn't it? You should add a man with a whip jumping over the words, and you on the racing tractor in hot pursuit, and me swooping in on a vine."

"A vine? Okay, *Tarzan*." She poked him playfully, nearly knocking him over.

"And maybe some flames! Flames are dangerous!"

His voice cracked in excitement. They both ignored it.

"I could do flames..." she trailed off thoughtfully. Fire had the intimidation factor she was looking for, and she'd seen enough wildfires to know how fast they could move. That was exactly the kind of thing she needed for Calamity: something that suggested speed and danger. "Fire it is. Thanks, Jet."

He nodded happily. "Don't mention it." Then he hunkered down in the dust to watch her as she painted. It had always been that way— Sally in the lead and Jet following dutifully along behind. Although Sally wouldn't have admitted it in public, she wouldn't have changed it for the world.

By the time the paint dried, they were late for the race, and Sally didn't want to give the gang any excuse to start without her. The neighborhood boys hadn't wanted to let her race in the first place until her brothers made them. Then she started winning, and everyone wanted her out. Even her brothers. But they couldn't oust her without losing face; it would mean they knew they could never beat her. And with Calamity on the track, they never would.

"We're late!" she shouted to Jet, leaping onto the seat. The well oiled springs jounced her gently to a stop, and she paused to inhale the familiar scent of kerosene and metal and paint. Not for the first time, she wished she could mechanize herself, become a metal girl full of gears and motors of infinite variation. But that was silly talk. She shook herself back to the present. There was a race to win. "Hop on!"

He leapt to the running board she'd installed on the side, clutching onto the back of her shoulder. "Calamity and Jet ride again!"

"Don't call me that," she said, turning the motor on with a satisfying hiss and rumble. "I'm Sally Slick, and someday everyone will know my name. I'm going to invent machines, and I'm going to be famous. Famouser than Calamity Sue ever was, even if she was a real person. Which she isn't."

"Whatever you say, Sal."

CHAPTER 2

Sally threw the racing tractor into gear. It accelerated smoothly due to her new piston design, with no lurch or bounce that might lose valuable seconds in a race. The engine purred. By this point, Sally was so excited that she couldn't help purring a little herself. No more fighting with her brothers for Pa's old tractor. It was about time; she'd been working on Calamity for almost a year-and-a-half. All that scrounging for parts, all the chores she'd traded for bits of metal, all the time spent repurposing parts meant for motorcars and railway trains—it was all finally going to pay off. She couldn't decide whether she wanted to shout or quake in her boots. She settled for driving like a maniac.

The dirt track where the kids of Nebraska Township, Illinois, gathered to race their tractors was only a mile away. Calamity kicked up a cloud of dust as they passed the mail carrier and his old horse-drawn buggy.

"Darned kids!" he yelled. Then he started coughing his lungs out.

"Hey, mister! Don't you know it's 1914? Get a motorcar, or get off the road!" Sally retorted, riding high on a wave of preemptive triumph.

"Sally," Jet hissed. "Be nice."

"I don't want to be nice." The words came out fierce as she hunched over the steering wheel. "And I don't want to be a proper young lady either. I'm tired of being told what I can and cannot do!"

"I wasn't telling you anything like that."

"Yeah, well..." Sally trailed off. Her palms were wet, and once she stopped to think about it, she realized she was scared. What if this didn't work—if Calamity didn't fly off the starting line like she was supposed to? It meant she was nothing special. She'd never go anywhere other than Nebraska Township; her dreams of adventure would amount to nothing. Her whole world hinged on the outcome of this race, and the pressure was getting to her. "Sorry," she mumbled.

"Don't mention it," he replied cheerily. "You're gonna knock 'em dead, kid."

"*Don't* call me 'kid.'"

When she turned down the lane and crested the hill that bordered the track, her heart sank. Everyone else was already there—about twenty boys ranging from age ten to eighteen—clustered around four racing tractors. As she roared up, the boys tilted their hats back, chewed blades of grass, and threw looks of skepticism her way, but she was used to that. She figured it was only to be expected when you were the only girl in a group of boys, and you had a tendency to beat them.

She pulled to a stop beside the twins, Isaiah and Henry. Henry stuck his tongue out and crossed his eyes. He was barely a year older than her, but he made a show of it whenever possible. Probably because he was the youngest of her brothers—other than the new baby—and she was the only person he could pick on without getting pummeled. It was kind of funny sometimes. The rest of the time, she wanted to knock his block off. But today, she had bigger things to think about.

"I'm not too late to get into the race, am I?" asked Sally.

Isaiah checked his notepad. Regardless of the number of racers, he carefully scheduled and organized each tractor race, compiling statistics and calculating odds. No project could go wrong with Isaiah's planning at the helm. Pa had even begun to use his new crop rotation plan, making him the only farmer in their township who took orders from a fifteen-year-old. It would have made him a laughingstock if yields hadn't gone up 25%. As it stood, the rest of the town wanted on board with the new system.

"No," he said slowly. "I don't suppose you are."

"She's late! She can't get in!"

Eugene Falks stomped over with his thumbs in the pockets of his overalls and a scowl on his lean, horsey face. He was taller than most men, even though he was the same age as the twins, and infamous for making his classmates eat dirt when the teachers weren't looking. He picked on Jet a lot, because no matter how many times Sally told Jet to avoid the Falks Gang like the plague, he refused to listen. Eugene would start picking on some younger kid, and before she knew it, Jet was there trying to stop him. It was brave, sure, but what kind of loony keeps picking fights he can never win?

So Eugene would pound Jet into pulp, and then he'd pound the little kid too, and nothing would be gained. She hated it, but what could she do? Falks and his gang already had it in for her for some unknown reason. The best thing to do was stay under the radar, even if she hated herself for it.

But now that she was behind the wheel of Calamity? For the first time, she found herself telling Eugene Falks exactly what was on her mind.

"You're just worried you'll eat my dust again, Falks," she said. "And with Calamity up and running, you just might."

He gaped. So did the rest of the boys, even the ones too old to be pushed around by the Falks Gang. They probably would have been less surprised if she'd grown a second head. No one talked to Eugene Falks like that, and especially not some scrawny, pigtailed girl in her brother's hand-me-down overalls.

She took advantage of the shock to press on. "Come on; sign me up."

"She missed the sign in," Eugene said to Isaiah, turning his back on her. "You know the rules."

"Well..." Isaiah said, drawing out the word uncertainly.

The argument was drawing attention, or maybe everyone just wanted a good look at Calamity. Sally hadn't let anyone other than Jet see the tractor before she was done, although she was pretty sure her brothers had snuck into the workshop for a peek at some point. Her sixteen-year-old brother, Wil, had a knack with simple mechanics. There wasn't a lock he couldn't pick if you gave him enough time. Regardless, the rest of the boys kept drifting closer and closer like they were in the grips of an out-of-control Hoover vacuum.

"It's too late," Eugene persisted. "Disqualified."

Henry stuck his tongue out at Eugene too. If he wasn't her brother, Sally would have hugged him.

"There's a rule..." Isaiah trailed off again, looking between Eugene's ruddy face and Sally's blotchy one.

"You haven't even lined up yet!" she exclaimed. "This is stupid! If you'd already started, fine, but all you were doing was sitting around and scratching your bottoms like Neanderthals!"

"Hey!" Wil stepped up and smacked her on the back of the head. "Button your lip, missy."

"Who are you calling 'missy'?" demanded Sally.

"The rules state..." Isaiah tried to break in.

"If she's in, I'm not racing. Who's with me?" Eugene exclaimed.

Everyone fell silent just in time to hear Jet murmur under his breath, "His own mom's not with him." After a moment of shocked silence, snickers began to spread through the crowd. Henry laughed so hard that something came out his nose, and that only made them laugh harder.

Even Sally began to giggle until Eugene took one step forward, cocked an arm, and punched Jet right in the mouth. It wasn't a weak love tap, either. This was a full-on, cock-the-arm, strike-hard-enough-to-knock-the-head-back punch. The back of Jet's skull banged into the flames on Calamity's side. There was a loud clang as his head struck the iron casing, and then he crumpled to the ground, blood spurting from his nose.

"You...you dirty rotten louse!" Sally shrieked, her fists clenched. She'd never been so angry before. Sure, she knew confronting Eugene was one of the stupidest things she'd ever done, but she couldn't help herself. Her arms felt like lead, and once again she wished for hands of metal just so she could bash his teeth in. The whole world narrowed until it was just her and her target, and she shook with adrenaline. "I'm gonna teach you a lesson."

"You and what army, you pantywaist?" Eugene leered down at her. And yes, he was twice her size, and no, she'd never been in a real fight before, but she'd had it. Someone had to stand up to him, and if no one else was going to do it, it would just have to be her.

"Stop," Jet mumbled, pushing up weakly from the ground. It sounded like he was talking through a mouthful of jam, and gore streaked his face. His split lip had already begun to puff up like a balloon. Tears streaked down his face; lines of blood segmented his shirt. It was not a pretty picture.

"I'm tired of him picking on people. I'm tired of running scared." The words tumbled out of Sally's mouth, furious and unstoppable. "I'm tired of waiting for somebody else to do something. Because none of you will." She glared at the boys assembled in a semi-circle, jostling for the best view of the fight to come. The Falks Gang—all three of them—just grinned at her, but some of the other boys had the decency to look ashamed. Her brothers shuffled their feet and looked sheepish until her brother John finally stepped forward. With James in the city looking for work, he was the eldest. He rarely exercised the power that came with that, but when he did, his word was law.

"That's enough, Sally," he said. The words came out gentle, but with finality. "Jet needs patching up. Go and take care of him."

"Why? Because I'm a *girl*? I'm so sick of—"

He broke in before she could wind herself up into a frenzy again. "No, because you're his *friend*. Isn't that more important than vengeance?"

"But..." She trailed off weakly. She hated that Eugene was getting away with the same old garbage again, but John had a point. This wasn't about what she wanted. It was about the kid at her feet with a probably-broken nose, and he needed help, and that's what heroes did, wasn't it? They did what needed doing. So although it stung her pride, she backed off, dropping down to a crouch beside Jet and helping him up. Blood still streamed out of his nose, so she pulled a spare handkerchief from her pocket. It was streaked with black smudges of oil, but it was better than nothing. She handed it to him.

"Yeah, tough girl," said Eugene. "Go put on your apron and take care of the baby. We don't want you here anyway."

"I forgot my apron," she shot back. "Can I borrow yours, pansy?"

"I'm gonna..." He thrust forward, fists cocked for another go, but this time her brothers got in the way. John grabbed one of his arms and Carl the other. The twins stepped into the space between Eugene and Sally, and Wil shoved her toward Calamity's driver's seat.

"I think now would be a good time to get out of here," he said. "Jet, can you hold on right here so you don't get thrown off?" He guided Jet's hand to the shiny steel bar that ran across the back of the seat.

Jet blinked his watery eyes, which were already beginning to swell along with his mouth, and nodded. He said something that sounded like: "Sure. Thanks."

"Good. Now skedaddle," Wil said. "We'll make sure Eugene knows he won't get away with that again."

Sally shook her head, but she started the engine. Her brothers meant well, but they just didn't understand. Their display of power here meant that she and Jet would have to watch their backs even more now. Her brothers couldn't protect them every second, and even if they could, she wouldn't have asked them to. That wasn't life. And Eugene wasn't going to stop until Sally and Jet stood up to him for real. She realized that now. He was the kind of boy who fed on fear, and she was tired of being scared.

But that would have to wait for the moment. She buried the pedal, and Calamity surged forward. The boys scattered out of the way, while Eugene and his buddies jeered and laughed.

"Coward! Sissy!" they called.

"Don't listen to them," Jet said, his consonants turning into mush in his damaged mouth.

It took her a moment to figure out what he'd said, and then she shrugged. "'Course I won't." But she was lying. Deep down, she wondered if maybe she *was* a coward. Because she'd talked the talk, but did that really count if you didn't walk the walk along with it?

CHAPTER 3

Back in the workshop, Sally applied about five minutes of constant pressure before Jet's nose quit gushing. Finally, she tossed the red-blotched bandanna onto her work table and surveyed the damage. It looked like he'd taken a train to the face. One tooth was chipped, and his nose was almost certainly broken. His left eye was still swollen despite a cold compress; bruises already carved half circles under his eyes. Yet, despite all that, he kept smiling at her. Maybe everyone was right about him. Because only a simp would be happy after what had just happened.

"Okay," she huffed. "I have got to know what you're grinning at. Because you're starting to worry me."

"You stood up for me, Sal." He shrugged, suddenly looking more than a little awkward. "That was nice. Nobody's ever really done that before."

"Don't be silly," she said. "Of course they have."

He shook his head. "Nope."

She opened her mouth to argue and then shut it again. Sure, she'd been there for Jet throughout the years, but mostly after the fact. She'd find him after Eugene popped him one, and she'd distract him from the pain. On the weekends, she'd let him hide out in her workshop where the Falks Gang would never find him. She'd provided distraction and shelter, but had she ever really stood up to them? Nope. And Jet had gone to bat for her hundreds of times. When she'd wanted to learn how to rebuild an engine, and Pa had been too busy, Jet had taken her to his dad's garage and talked him into letting her help out. He'd spent tons of afternoons in her workshop even though he wasn't half as interested in inventing things as she was. He'd carted parts too big for her to manage on her own, tightened screws, and fetched lemonade from the house, all without complaint. All this time, she'd taken that for granted. Only now when her dream of racing Calamity was on the line did she realize how selfish she'd been. But it wasn't too late to fix, was it?

She looked out the window, listening for the faint rumble of tractor engines from far away. Her brothers still weren't home. Either they'd gotten into a scrap with Eugene and she and Jet were missing it, or the unthinkable had happened—they'd waited until she was gone and decided to race with him anyway. They'd swept it all under the rug. How could they do that to her? Weren't brothers supposed to stick up for their younger sisters? She would have stuck up for them. After the initial burst of anger, she settled into a cold determination. She'd been sweeping things under the rug for ages. It would end now.

"Come on," she said. "Bring one of those rags in case you blow a gasket."

"Huh?" Jet blinked at the dishcloths like one of them might develop the power of speech and translate what she just said.

"I've had enough of this. We're gonna take on Eugene, and we're gonna win."

"He's awful big, Sally."

"Maybe so, but Calamity's bigger."

Once he got the gist of what she was saying, he leapt up with his usual hyperactive excitement. "That's a dilly of an idea! What are you waiting for?"

The ride back to the track seemed to take forever, even though Calamity ate up the road at her usual speed. As they crested the hill for the second time that afternoon, Sally stood up in her seat, trying to get a better view of the race in progress. Henry was losing badly to one of Eugene's flunkies, but he'd never been the best driver. He really only raced because he liked to talk a bunch of jive to his opponents. He was all words and no action. It seemed to be a Slick family trait, but Sally was about to put an end to that.

The track cut a straight line across the unused field, a stretch of rocky ground too poor to grow anything on. String ran down the length of the track, tied to wooden stakes, and a row of spectators stood alongside it. As the tractors crossed the finish line, the boys traded Cracker Jack cards and candy buttons as bets were won and lost.

Eugene pulled up to the starting line, way off to Sally's left and almost in the trees. The Slick family tractor rumbled up alongside him, the same one Sally had raced until today. It was a good machine— she'd done all the maintenance work on it—but nothing compared to Calamity's speed. She was built to race, and to win.

There was no time to think. Sally threw Calamity into gear and rumbled onto the track. Eugene would have to take her challenge or roll right over her.

"Get out of the way, Sally!" yelled John. "We're trying to race!"

"Racing with that bully isn't right, and you know it!" she replied.

"He's going to leave you two alone from now on. He promised. Right, Eugene?"

"Yeah, of course." Eugene grinned wide. He looked like a hungry, horse-faced shark.

No one believed him. Jet and Sally exchanged a skeptical glance, which was mirrored by the rest of the group. She could tell from John's expression that he knew it just as well as anyone, but he was torn between the desire to race and the need to stick up for his kid sister.

"He broke Jet's nose," she said loudly. "That's not something you wave off. I'm not moving. Either race me, or try to run me off the track. I dare you." She felt fierce and reckless. "I double dog dare you."

"You've got a smart mouth for a girl," Eugene yelled back. "We'll see how smart it is after I shove my fist in it!"

Without realizing it, he'd stepped over a line. Her brothers closed in on the sides of Eugene's tractor, ready to take him down. Finally, they'd gotten the picture too. But it wasn't enough to have the Slick boys stop him. She had to do it if this was ever going to end.

"Stop!" she yelled. "He's mine. I'm gonna take him on."

Her brothers paused uncertainly. Had they heard her right? Because that was crazy talk.

"Mano-a-mano?" Eugene shouted back. "You don't stand a chance."

"Not mano-a-mano. Tracto-a-tracto."

He snorted, either at the phrase or the idea. Maybe both. "I'm not racing a skirt. Go cook something."

"Make me."

She folded her arms defiantly and settled back into her seat. Eugene couldn't back away from this challenge. He'd never live it down if he gave way to some girl. He'd have to go up against her, and then she'd win, and then he'd realize that she wasn't going to roll over and show her belly anymore. It was going to work. It had to.

He threw his tractor into gear with a lurch and a rumble, and it started down the track toward her. John stood up in his seat as Eugene rolled past, shouting for him to stop, but Eugene just grinned at him.

The spectators started to shout encouragement as the tractor rolled down the pitted dirt, about fifty yards from Calamity's exposed flank.

Jet squinted toward the oncoming vehicle—or maybe that was just the swelling—and let out a single nervous bleat. "Uh...Sally?"

"On it."

Without even thinking, she twisted the wheel, bringing Calamity around and onto the racing track. But she didn't flee. She'd said she was done with that, and she'd meant it. She aimed Calamity toward Eugene's tractor on a collision course. Falks blanched and then glared at her like that might make his clunking machine move faster.

"I'll mow you down, Sally!" he yelled.

"Fat chance, buster!" she replied.

"Are you sure this is a good idea?" Jet muttered.

She glanced at him. "Don't worry," she said. "Calamity's up to this. Trust me."

He nodded shortly and shifted his grip, his knuckles going white as he clutched at the back of her seat. It felt good to be trusted, because now that she'd committed to this course of action, a little voice inside her head began to question her sanity. If Eugene didn't turn aside, they would crash. And if she wrecked Calamity on her first day out of the workshop, Sally was going to lock herself in her room for the rest of eternity, because it meant that her life was over.

But turning away was unthinkable. She would do this, if not for herself, then for Jet. Because friends stick together, and believing that wasn't enough. It was past time for her to put it into action regardless of the consequences.

So she squinted into the clouds of dust hovering over the track, watching as Eugene drew closer. The tractors ate up the ground, churning divots into the hard-packed dirt. Forty yards. The onlookers began to shout excitedly at one another, placing bets on whether they'd collide, or whether one of the drivers would pull off the track and risk tumbling sideways into the drainage ditch that ran along it. Thirty yards. Calamity's rumble no longer felt soothing. It felt to Sally like she was being marched to her death, and the fear must have shown on her face. Eugene was laughing.

"Dumb girl! You don't have the guts," he said.

"Screw you!" yelled Jet gleefully. "Eat tractor, Falks!"

He began bouncing on the baseboard, his eyes bright. Or at least they seemed to be, from what she could see of them. They were mostly swollen shut by now. But his grin was unmistakable, and regardless of what happened, it felt like she'd won something. Sally hunched over the gear shift, as if leaning forward might increase Calamity's momentum. Jet believed in her. Why couldn't she?

Ten yards.

She could see the sweat tracks on Eugene's forehead, inching their way through the dust that clung to his skin. His triumphant grin began to falter, and she hoped against hope that he might clear out. She could finish the ride a winner without damage to Calamity. But he didn't pull off to the side.

Eight yards. Five. He still didn't pull off the track, and she wasn't going to give him the satisfaction of turning away, and then it was too late for either of them to reconsider. His eyes widened in surprise, and then the tractors collided.

Sally had made many changes to Calamity. Some of them were for comfort, like adding shocks and tooled leather to the seat. Some were for speed, like her improved engine design. But the stability modifications saved her and Jet at that moment. Calamity sat low to the ground, more stable than Eugene's regular old farm tractor.

The two machines hit with a screech of metal that sent hands flying to ears, and then there was a scrape as Calamity kept on going. Eugene's lighter machine went up on its back wheels with a tortured squeal, leaving long divots in the ground. As the machine tilted, he was thrown from the seat and straight into the drainage ditch. There hadn't been much rain, so he didn't get wet, but there was a loud thump as he landed so maybe that wasn't such a good thing after all.

But Sally didn't have much time to think about that, because she was currently pushing Eugene's tractor back toward the starting line on two wheels, and the sound of protesting metal was only getting louder. She didn't want to permanently damage Calamity's front grill. So she threw it into reverse. Calamity backed away with another screech, leaving Eugene's tractor up on one end. It wiggled back and forth on its rear wheels like a hyperactive puppy. That mental picture made Sally break out into hysterical giggles.

She'd tested Calamity and had been tested herself, and neither of them had failed.

Jet threw his arms around her before realizing that they were the center of attention and then released her hastily. But the boys didn't even seem to notice his embarrassing gesture of affection. They were too busy trying to get the goods on Calamity.

"Where'd you get the name, Sally?" said one.

"Did you do all the work yourself?" added another.

"I bet she didn't."

"She's been working with Old Man Black over at the service station, blockhead!" Henry butted in, looking more proud than he had any right to, since he hadn't done anything to contribute to Calamity's design. "Of course she did it all herself. She's a Slick, and there ain't nothing we can't build."

"Yeah?" John sounded amused. "When's the last time you built something, huh?"

Henry sputtered but didn't manage to get anything out.

"That's what I thought. Let Sally talk. She's the one who put the work in."

He turned to her with an expression of respect, and suddenly Sally found herself at the center of a circle of rapt attention. Her cheeks colored as she began to explain Calamity's design, and Jet settled into the seat with an expression of satisfaction, lacing his hands behind his head. She talked long after Calamity's engine finished ticking. At some point, Eugene dragged himself out of the drainage ditch, the seat of his pants ripped from his abrupt landing. He limped on home to change. No one even noticed.

CHAPTER 4

By the time she made it home from the impromptu game of tractor chicken, Sally was exhausted from all the excitement and ready to
tear into a different kind of fowl—some of Ma's famous chicken and
biscuits. But when she opened the screen door and burst into the mud
room, there were no welcoming lights from the kitchen, no tantalizing
wafts of yeasty air that promised fresh baked goods to come. The house
was as silent as a tomb.

"Oh no," she moaned, leaning her grimy head against the wall and
nearly impaling her eyeball on one of the coat hooks. "This is not
good."

"What's up?" Her brother Carl came through the door behind
her, tossing his coat in the general vicinity of his hook and missing it
entirely. That didn't seem to bother him. "You look worried."

"Do you smell dinner?" she demanded.

He paused to sniff the air and then groaned too. "Oh no," he echoed.
"Exactly."

They made their way into the kitchen, but it was empty just as they'd expected. The lamps were unlit, the stove unheated. A bowl of dough sat rising under a towel with a handwritten list of instructions at its side. One look at that list was enough to turn the excited fizzy feeling in Sally's stomach to lead.

"What's for dinner?" Henry asked, bursting into the kitchen behind them.

"Sally's cooking," said Carl, with the kind of funereal voice most often used to tell people their cat died.

"Oh no!" exclaimed Henry. Even though Sally had already said the same thing, she kind of wanted to punch him right then.

"Well, there's no use griping about it now," she said. "Go out and fetch me some water and then get out of my way."

For a moment, it looked like they might argue, but one look at her face convinced them it wasn't a good idea. They grabbed the metal buckets by the back door and took them out to the pump while Sally surveyed the instructions Ma had left in her note. It wasn't quite as bad as she'd thought. The chicken was plucked and the potatoes already peeled and soaking in a bowl of cold water. The biscuit dough was mixed and covered with a towel. It was just a matter of heating everything up, and she wasn't a terrible cook or anything, but she didn't much like doing it.

She'd been helping out at home more and more often since Ralphie was born. He'd been a surprise from the beginning, and then he'd come early, and he'd been sick ever since. Over the past month, he'd been making this barking noise like a dog, so loud it kept everyone up at night until Ma started taking him out of the house during his coughing fits. The cold air seemed to help him rest, and everyone else slept better, but Ma had gotten more and more gray-faced and exhausted with every day that passed. Last week, she'd started taking naps every time the baby slept. And that left Sally to fill in the gaps.

She understood why all of this was happening, and of course she wanted Ma to get some sleep too, and she wanted her baby brother to be okay, and for everything to go back to the way it had been. She wanted Ma in the kitchen as usual, yelling at them all for tracking mud on her floors and then giving them cookies after they wiped up the mess. But that wasn't going to happen. They all just had to soldier through.

Biscuit dough doesn't require kneading, but she couldn't resist pretending it was Eugene's face and punching it a few times. Then the boys came in and sloshed water all over the floor, and that gave her something to complain about, which was kind of fun too. Then, still high off her victory with Calamity, she realized that the stovepipe would work so much better with only a few minor adjustments, which she could easily make while the biscuits were cooking, and by the time she was done with that, she realized she'd forgotten to put the chicken in. By the time she finished dashing around and putting everything into the pot, big plumes of smoke were coming out of the oven. She burnt her hand on the door when she pulled the biscuits out. They looked more like coal than biscuits, but there was nothing to be done about that now. She set them on the porch to cool while she set the table and finally called the rest of the boys in.

"Dinner!" she yelled, feeling sweaty and exhausted and discouraged. After her wave of triumph that afternoon, it really stunk that this meal had to come along and ruin it. She didn't want to face the complaints. And besides, she was *starving*.

Her brothers filed in with expressions of stoic resolve, and from the way John was giving everyone the stink eye, it was clear that he'd sent the edict out—no complaints. They helped themselves to rubbery chicken, undercooked potatoes, and blackened biscuits without a peep. She shot her older brother a grateful glance as she made up a plate for Ma with the best of the food. Pa had gone to Greenfield for the calving auction and wouldn't be back for another couple of days, so at least she didn't have to worry about subjecting him to the food.

The dinner was actually a triumph despite itself; everyone was starving, and with enough butter on top of it, the food underneath became irrelevant. But when the door opened again, Sally's heart sank. If it was anyone but Jet, she was going to scream out of frustration.

It wasn't Jet, and she did scream, but it was out of surprise. Her eldest brother James ambled into the room, thumbs hooked into the pockets of his suit coat. He looked years older than he had when he'd left only a few months earlier—like a real grown up with a pocket watch and everything. Even his hair was different. The Slick boys all wore their sandy hair a little long; it was shaggy-looking but kept them from developing cowlicks. In contrast, James had cut his into a short bristle. It made him look like one of the evil Feds from Sally's favorite book, *Astonishing Adventures*.

"James!" Everyone greeted him, but it was Henry who leapt out of his chair and tried to lock him in a half Nelson. James shrugged him off and cuffed him on the back of the head amiably enough, but he didn't smile.

Sally pulled a lock of her own sandy hair out of the kerchief that held it out of her face and chewed nervously on the end. James was supposed to be working in Chicago. He'd saved up for years to make enough money to move there, thinking he might get a factory job or work at the train yard. Farm life had never suited him; it was too quiet. James needed excitement and bustle to keep him entertained, and the house had been much more peaceful without him. At least until the barking baby had come along.

"Is there enough for me, Sally?" James asked, as if it were completely normal to find his sister at the stove, the kitchen hazy from smoke, and their mother nowhere to be found. The rest of the family was used to it, but he'd left home shortly before Ralphie was born. The fact that he seemed to find Sally's cookery unremarkable was...weird. He'd always been a complainer. She hadn't minded seeing the back of him when he'd left, except that he was the only one who had taken her plans to build a racing tractor seriously. Occasionally, he'd surprise people that way, popping out to do something really nice and then going back to his usual self. Maybe he was in one of his rare good moods. Maybe the city had changed him. "I'd love some dinner," he added.

"If you're up for the risk," she said with uncharacteristic honesty.

He shrugged. "I'm a bachelor who lives alone in a big city. If it's not tinned, it's a treat."

"You say that now..." Isaiah cautioned. Sally threw a biscuit at him. It ricocheted off his forehead, leaving a sooty circle in its wake. He grinned as he picked it up off the floor, blew on it, and then began to cover the entire surface with butter. "If the biscuit fits..." he added.

She snorted and began making up a plate for James. He sat down at the head of the table, in Pa's seat, shrugged off his jacket and rolled up his shirtsleeves.

"So it's not like we're not happy to see you," Sally said, "but what are you doing here?"

"Didja get a cool job?" added Henry.

"Do you have a girl?" Carl asked.

"I'm working," James said coolly, like it was no big deal. "How else do you think I bought this suit?"

"Swanky." Carl rubbed the sleeve between his two fingers. "I bet it cost you a pretty penny. Once I graduate, I'm gonna see if Pa will let me go to the city, too. Maybe you can get me a job."

"Pa will be glad to see you go," Henry said. "You're too much of a pretty boy to get your hands dirty."

"Shut up, lunkhead," Carl said, but he seemed more flattered than insulted. He'd always been a bit of a dandy. Sally didn't get his fascination with the outsides of stuff when the insides were so cool, but he was really good with the appearance of a thing. She bet he would have figured out Calamity's paint design without any help at all.

The thought of Calamity brought back the rush of the race. James had started the races in the first place, and he'd given her the idea to build Calamity, even if he hadn't taken it seriously at the time. He'd be pleased to hear how it had all turned out. As she placed his plate on the table, she said, "You won't believe what happened today. It was race day, and I finally finished my new tractor after almost a year-and-a-half of scrounging up the parts, and Eugene Falks was there, and you know how he is." She rolled her eyes. "Anyway, he picked a fight with Jet, and..."

She continued telling the story as she began clearing the table, but right about the time she got to the point where Eugene's tractor capsized, she realized he was saying things like, "Uh huh," and "You don't say," but not actually listening to a single word. He'd fixated on his plate instead, shoveling food into his mouth without even seeming to taste it. Maybe he really was starving. She couldn't decide whether to be angry or worried, but she couldn't shake the instinctive feeling that something was wrong.

"James," she asked softly, "are you in trouble?"

Sally wasn't sure what got everyone's attention, the content of the question or the fact that gentleness wasn't something usually associated with Sally Slick. Not that she couldn't be kind, but in a house full of boys, you had to speak up or get run over. That was usually true, anyway, but not this time. The whole room froze like the belt on the engine of time just broke.

The question shocked James too. Momentarily, his eyes flicked up to hers, and she could swear she saw panic deep inside them. His shoulders drew up defensively, ready to hide. When the blow didn't come, the fear was quickly replaced with defensive anger.

"You don't know what you're talking about," he snapped.

Normally, this was the kind of challenge Sally rose to. She could argue and shout with the best of them, and she'd be darned if she'd let one of her brothers run all over her because she was younger or because she was a girl. But this time, something made her pause. James had always pushed her buttons, but it was because he'd ignored her entirely and that hurt her feelings. He'd never been the kind of person who started arguments; he couldn't be bothered to care enough to make the effort.

There was only one conclusion: he was trying to pick a fight. He wanted her mad. Because if she got angry, she wouldn't pursue the big questions. Because she'd forget that he'd never said why he'd come home.

So she took a deep breath and let it out, trying to focus the same way she did in the workshop when her latest machinery design wasn't quite working the way she wanted. Hey, the technique had worked the few times Ma had left her with the baby, so it had to be good for something. Hopefully James wasn't about to throw up on her face like Ralphie had.

She shrugged. "Maybe. Maybe not," she said. Then she began to fill the wash basin before he could continue trying to pick a fight. Or vomit.

It worked better than she'd expected. He didn't know what to make of her lack of response, and she heard him muttering as his chair scraped along the floor. By the time she turned around, he'd gotten up from the table and left the room.

"Well, that was weird," she said.

Most of the boys ignored her, still busy trying to pick off the edible bits from the chicken. But Isaiah met her eyes and nodded slowly. He looked as worried as she felt, but neither of them followed James. Not then, anyway.

CHAPTER 5

At first, she thought it was the cat. Sally awoke in the dark of the night with a start, her heart pounding as her mind tried to catch up with the sound her ears had already heard. After a panicked moment during which she fully expected a masked assassin to pop out of her closet, she settled back into the fluffy down of her pillow with a chuckle. Gadget had the habit of pawing at the door and then running off. Stupid cat. She pulled her quilt up over her shoulder and flipped over, wriggling into the warm depths of the bed.

"Damn!"

The curse was muffled but unmistakable. And unless Gadget had developed the power to speak English, it meant that she'd been wrong about the source of the noise. Now she was curious. She crept out of bed to the open window of her second story bedroom. The linen curtains ballooned gently in the cool nighttime breeze. She peeked out from behind them, searching the front yard for signs of an intruder. She kept a long wrench under her bed to discourage Henry from playing nighttime pranks on her. If somebody was trying to break into their house, she'd give them what for.

But instead of someone trying to enter their house, the full moon illuminated a figure rushing away from the door towards the barn. At first, she figured it was just Henry, up to his usual shenanigans. One time, she'd gone in to feed the chickens in the morning only to be greeted by a stuffed dummy hanging from the rafters. It probably would have been scarier if one of the hens hadn't been perched on top of its head, flapping and squawking in complete hysteria. As it was, she'd laughed until tears came out her eyes.

But when the person glanced nervously toward the house, she didn't see Henry's usual cat-with-the-canary-feather grin. It was James, and he definitely wasn't smiling. He hunched into the collar of his shirt and slunk into the tool shed.

After a moment's hesitation, she grabbed the wrench from under the bed, pulled a robe on over her nightgown, and crept down the stairs. He'd had it much easier; his old bedroom was on the first floor. No creaky stairs to give him away. She made it about halfway down the steps, wincing at every sound, when the baby began coughing again. That made her feel pretty guilty, especially when she heard the dull, sleep-deepened tones of her mother's voice trying to soothe him, but not so guilty that she didn't take advantage of the covering noise and hustle down the steps.

She threw her boots on without socks, convinced that at any moment someone would light the kitchen lamp and demand to know what she was doing out here in the middle of the night. She couldn't even claim to be on a hunt for cookies, because Ma hadn't baked any in weeks. The outhouse wasn't in the middle of the front yard, so she couldn't claim to be on her way there. Maybe they'd believe she was sleepwalking? She put her hands out in front of her and half closed her eyes to make the story seem more plausible, but then she bumped the door frame with her shoulder so she stopped.

The night had seemed quiet from her bedroom, but once she was outside the door, she couldn't stop twitching from all the ruckus. The moon lit the lawn just enough to make the tree line look extra ominous. At the edge of the porch, the flapping wings of a hunting owl or bat made her jump. Two steps onto the lawn, and the scree-scree of crickets startled her. A twig snapped somewhere in the woods off to the side of the house, and even though she knew it was probably just a deer, she clutched the wrench hard, trying to get her heart out of her throat. But it was stuck there.

The shed door stood open, and a quick peek around it was enough to confirm that her brother was no longer inside. Where had he gone? She couldn't see hide nor hair of him, and she hurried around to the side of the house in the vain hope that she'd catch sight of him. But with the head start he'd had? There was no telling where he'd gone.

If it wasn't for his habit of not cleaning up for himself, she never would have found him. But the door to her workshop stood open, and she was always careful to close it tight lest the raccoons try to build another nest in there. She crept up to the open door and peeked inside. If he was messing with Calamity...but the workshop was still and silent. He'd walked out through that seldom-used door on the other end—it stood open, too. So with a deep yet unsuccessful calming breath, she followed him.

This path led only two places, and there was no good reason to go to either of them in the middle of the night. One was a field full of potatoes. The other was the family graveyard. Three generations of Slicks were buried there, marked by stones in varying stages of decay. Sally didn't go there much. She wasn't a fraidy cat or anything, but dead people still gave her the jitters.

She followed him down the path, taking note of the broken branches along the path and the long furrows on the ground. The moonlight was scattered here, but the marks of his passage were impossible to miss.

There was no question he'd gone this way, but why? He must have been dragging something heavy, something big. What was it? At least he wasn't coming from the graveyard with a sack of bones. Even though she knew it was ridiculous, the thought made her shudder.

She was so lost in thought that she almost caught up to him. The path curved and twisted through the trees like a directionally challenged snake, and she rounded a moss-covered trunk to see him standing only a few yards away. She froze in place, but he was distracted by the handful of shovels he was juggling. He dropped two of them before managing to open the wooden gate of the cemetery with a creak. By this time, they were far from the house, and he must have been pretty confident because he didn't turn back to see if anyone had heard the noise. That was a good thing, because Sally found herself standing out in full sight, too terrified to move.

Inside the cemetery, James began to organize his equipment, making enough noise that Sally worried someone from the house really might hear them even though they were clearly too far away. She scrambled into a convenient maple to get out of the path just in case. Unfortunately, taking cover screwed up the view. She tried to figure out what on earth he was doing, but it was hard to tell because the trees blocked her line of sight. But then James walked out into a clear patch with a shovel over one arm; it glinted as the light hit the blade. Then he began to dig.

At first Sally was relieved, because if her brother had turned out to be a grave robber, she didn't know what she would have done. Then she grew puzzled, because of course they'd dug graves here before, but no one in the family had died. And if he was trying to make a comment on Ralphie's health and well-being, she was going to box his ears, because that was just horrible. There was no good reason for James to be digging graves in the middle of the night. If he couldn't sleep and needed some exercise to relax, there were plenty of other things he could have tried. Isaiah sometimes went outside and ran laps around the house when he was thinking too hard to rest, and that usually worked for him.

But then she realized that maybe this wasn't a grave at all. Maybe he was burying treasure! He'd found it while he was in Chicago, and then he brought it here to keep it safe, and...

No, that didn't make sense either. It didn't add up no matter how she sliced it. Because if he'd just *found* the treasure, why would he need to hide it? The only reason to hide something in a graveyard in the middle of the night was if you'd stolen it.

It was a horrible thing to think about your own kin, but she couldn't think of any other explanation that made sense. That would explain why he'd been so cagey at dinner. He'd swiped something but was too scared to admit it. She scowled down at him, preparing to jump from the tree and demand that he give whatever it was back to the person who rightfully owned it.

But then he opened the sack to reveal a random collection of garden implements—shovels and a pick and clippers—and set them on the ground near an unused plot. Sally felt a wave of confused relief right up until the moment he began to haul a mysterious bundle off Pa's favorite wheelbarrow toward the empty space. Whatever it was, the thing was heavy. It moved inch by arduous inch, and James grunted with the strain. A bunch of old horse blankets swaddled the whatever-it-was, but there was still no mistaking the outline of two legs, a pair of arms, a long torso, and a lumpy misshapen head. For a moment, Sally couldn't believe what she was seeing. Then she felt scared, followed quickly by a wave of fury. How dare her brother bury someone in their family graveyard in the middle of the night?! If Pa found out, he'd get the belt for sure. Frankly, James was lucky *she* wasn't wearing a belt, because she'd use it to swing out of the tree like Tarzan and kick him in the face.

Instead, she had to settle for leaping out of the tree, howling like an enraged banshee, and getting the hem of her nightgown snagged on a pricker bush before she could land a blow. James stood there gaping at her like she was the crazy one. It only served to make her angrier.

"How dare you?" she demanded, tugging at her gown. This was why she kept asking Ma for sleeping pants, except Ma said only floozies wore those. Sally didn't know exactly what a floozie was, but she bet they didn't get stuck in pricker bushes while trying to ambush killers in the middle of the night.

That thought made her pause, and she looked at her brother again cautiously. He was still frozen with the shovel resting on one shoulder, but that wasn't going to last long. And the fact that he was burying a dead guy in the middle of the night raised one important question— how had the guy gotten dead in the first place? Had he done it?

"Ma!" she shrieked. "Anybody! Come quick! James is burying someone in the graveyard!"

James leapt toward her with a muffled oath, and she tore her night-gown free of the prickers, leaving a big swatch of faded linen stuck there, waving like a flag of surrender. She whirled to flee, still shrieking with all her might even though she knew they were too deep in the woods to be easily heard from the house. But maybe Ma was still awake with Ralphie. Maybe she'd hear before it was too late and Sally ended up dead, too. She figured someday she'd be buried in this graveyard, but not yet. She wasn't ready to die! She hadn't even really gotten to race Calamity yet.

"Will you shut up?" James demanded as he scrambled after her.

"Leave me alone!" she yelled, and then her wild flight took her right over a fallen branch. It caught her ankle, and the world flipped upside down. She hit the path with her face. Leaves filled her mouth, muffling her screams. But she definitely screamed, especially when James leapt on top of her.

"Shut. Up."

He clapped a hand over her face, which wouldn't have felt good under any circumstances, but really hurt when you considered that she'd almost gouged a hole to China in the ground with her chin. She retaliated with a flailing elbow. She'd never been much of a fighter, but as the smallest sibling, she'd mastered the cat-in-a-bathtub technique. For some reason, she managed to land more blows that way. This time, she got him squarely in the stomach, and he released her abruptly with a sound somewhere between *oof* and *ugh*. He sounded like a very confused caveman. If she hadn't had such a case of the willies, she might have laughed.

Then a bright glint on the path caught her eye. Her wrench! She'd forgotten all about it in the shock of seeing the dead body and must have dropped it on the ground. But it wasn't too far. She scrambled for it, spitting dirt and leaves and other things she'd rather not think about out of her mouth. The moment her fingers touched the smooth, cool metal, she felt better. She whirled around, cocking the wrench at the ready.

But instead of attacking her, James gave her a wounded look. This seemed backwards to Sally. Was he honestly upset that she'd ruined his attempt at getting away with a crime, and if so, how dangerous would it be to laugh at him?

"Well?" she demanded. "What are you waiting for?"

"Uh..." He blinked. "I'm not sure. You're not going to throw that at me, are you?"

"Why shouldn't I?"

"Well, because I'm your *brother* for starters. That should make me exempt from the whole leaping out of a tree to attack people in the middle of the night with a wrench bit, don't you think?"

"So you think *I'm* in the wrong here?" Sally couldn't believe what she was hearing, and by this time she was so mad that she was pretty sure smoke was coming out her ears. "Of all the nerve!"

"My nerve? What about yours? You tried to knock my block off!"

"You deserved it, murderer!"

He stopped, his mouth falling open, and then inexplicably began to laugh. "You think..." he gasped out, "that I... really?!"

"What about murder is funny, James?" she asked coldly.

"I didn't murder anybody. See for yourself."

He backed up a few steps and crouched by the figure on the ground, snatching the burlap off and tossing it to the side. She couldn't help it; curiosity got the better of her, and she stood up to get a better look. It was humanoid for sure, but the moonlight glinted off the creature's metallic skin. It clearly wasn't human, which meant that she wasn't related to a killer. The feeling of relief that washed over her was so strong that she staggered.

But that feeling was quickly overcome by curiosity. She crept across the grave of Great Aunt Agnes—who had always smelled like boiled cabbage—to get a better look at the metal man.

CHAPTER 6

Sally crept toward the metal figure on the ground. It was probably a suit of armor; she knew that was the most likely explanation. But she'd seen pictures of armor before, and this didn't look like anything the Knights of the Round Table would have worn. There wasn't an air vent for starters, just an indented line where the mouth should have been. A knight would have lasted about a minute before he fell over from lack of oxygen.

But if it wasn't armor, what was it?

One glance, and she knew. This wasn't just some empty hunk of metal; this was a machine. Vacuum tubes ran across the joints, providing pressure to power movement. Each joint was a carefully constructed set of metal plates that she ached to take apart. It reminded her of a china doll; she'd had one once—from Great Aunt Agnes of the cabbage smell, in fact—only this thing was much cooler. Unlit orange glass suggested eyes in a can shaped head. An antenna rose from its temple, searching for...what? Was it a giant radio receiver shaped like a person? But why would anyone build something like that?

"It's broken," James said glumly.

"What is it?" she demanded. "I don't understand."

"This is BEM. He's a Bipedal Energetic Mechanism." He dug through the burlap, looking for something swaddled in its folds. "This is supposed to control him, but I can't make it work."

She snatched at the small black box he held out toward her. It was a simple controller with a radio dial and a series of switches topped by lights, all of which were dark. She couldn't help it. She flipped each of them and twisted the dial, and she could swear that the metal man's left leg twitched. Her stomach leapt; she couldn't keep a squeal of excitement from escaping her lips. But as soon as the movement began, it stopped, and the lights remained dark.

"Did that...?" She stared at BEM with wide eyes and began frantically flipping switches, but nothing happened.

"He walks, all by himself. And he can follow basic preprogrammed instructions," said James proudly. "That's what I've been working on for the past few months."

"I thought you worked in the train yard."

"Technically, I do. The doctor's lab is hidden at the back of the yard." He lifted his chin proudly. "But my work is secret, or at least it was until you barged in. Can you keep it quiet, Sal?"

She knew the use of her nickname was meant to flatter her, and she wasn't about to fall for that. She tossed her head, wisps of hair flopping immediately back into her eyes.

"You're kidding, right?" she exclaimed. "Not without an explanation. Because it seems to me that you wouldn't be hiding this thing if it was really yours. Why is it such a secret?"

"Because." He let out a huff of exasperated breath. "My boss sent me here to hide it, dummy."

"Why?"

"This thing is an important prototype. It's in demand; people have tried to take it from us already. You have no idea."

"Don't insult my intelligence, James. I built my racing tractor from the ground up. I know machines." Her chin lifted with pride.

"Yeah, well, I'm hiding this particular machine until I figure out what to do..." He trailed off, looking at her with a sudden, fierce intensity. "You really built a whole tractor on your own?"

"Yep. Designed it and everything."

"Maybe you could take a look at BEM," he said diffidently. "See if you can figure out what's wrong."

She wasn't sure what made him take her seriously, because he usually didn't. He was the eldest of the Slick brothers, and his job had always been to make sure she was solidly in her place. In the past few months since he'd left and Ralphie got sick, she'd gotten a little more responsibility, and with that came some respect. But by that time, James had already left for the city. He'd missed Calamity. He'd missed the time Jet's dad called her in to help repair Old Man Lewis's tractor. He still knew her as the pest, so this was a big deal.

"Wouldn't your boss be upset if I fooled with his...is BEM his name or what?" she asked tentatively.

"BEM is his model name. We're in the design process for BEM2 right now. Doktor Proktor calls them robots."

"Proktor?" She arched a brow. "The boss?"

He nodded.

"All right. I'll take a look at this robot-thing for you." She tried to sound confident and capable and not completely terrified. It failed entirely, but now that James had confided in her, it was pretty obvious that he was too relieved to notice. "He doesn't know it's broken, does he?"

"Huh?" He tried to look confused, but he clearly knew what she was talking about.

"Your boss. He doesn't know you broke his robot. Right?"

He shrugged, trying to look casual, but failed entirely. "Well, no. But he had to know that it might get damaged in transit. And it's still important that I keep it hidden. There are people...dangerous people. They'd kill for this design. In fact," he added darkly, "they already have."

"So you decided to bury it in the graveyard to keep it secret."

He nodded, and she was about to compliment him on his choice of hiding places. No one would think twice at finding upturned earth in a cemetery. Any of these "dangerous people" would completely overlook it as a potential hiding place. So as she began to pry open the back of the control device, she opened her mouth to tell him how smart she thought he was. But she got interrupted first.

"Too late."

The voice was gravel over smoke. At first, she looked down at the metal man—the robot—with wide eyes, expecting to see its mouth in motion. But of course it wasn't talking. The speaker was a man standing at the end of the cemetery, the moon at his back. A long, dark jacket widened his figure and a bowler topped his head. His face was cloaked in shadow, but his eyes glinted with a fey and dangerous light. Or maybe she just thought so because of the gun clutched in his hand.

Sally had never looked down the wrong end of a gun before, and it didn't feel good. The muzzle looked enormous. It seemed to swallow up the whole world. Her limbs froze, and even though she knew it would be really smart to throw the wrench at him and dive for cover or call for help or *something*, she couldn't manage to move an inch.

"Uh..." she said.

The gun wavered then and settled on James, dismissing her as a threat. She couldn't decide whether to be insulted or relieved.

"I'll take that," said the man with the gun, holding out a hand.

It seemed to Sally that the smart thing to do would be to hand over the control device, but James snatched it from her before she could make a move. He had that mulish expression she recognized all too well. It was the same expression he'd worn when he told Pa he was moving to the city and there wasn't anything anyone could say that would make him change his mind. Pa had known it was fruitless, but he'd tried anyway. He'd been counting on having the extra hand at the farm and maybe on passing the whole operation down to his eldest son. It had been a stressful few weeks in the Slick household until James left, and things still weren't quite the same. Pa kept staring at each of them like he expected them to suddenly sprout wings and fly the coop.

Sally hadn't planned to go anywhere, not yet anyway. She *definitely* hadn't planned to get shot in the family graveyard. It was up to her to make sure that it didn't happen. Now that the gun wasn't pointed at her, it was like her brain was working again. She began to edge backwards, evaluating her options for escape.

"You can't have it," James snapped. "It's mine."

"The BEM project was funded by the Steel Don, sonny," sneered the man. "It all belongs to him. And there isn't anything you or this miserable brat can do about it. Now hand it over. My trigger finger's getting tired."

"Um...James?" Sally asked nervously. "What's going on?"

"Not now, Sally." James glanced at her once and then reluctantly held out the control device. "I'll do it, Fat Lorenzo. Don't shoot us, okay? That's my kid sister."

Sally snorted. Fat Lorenzo? What kind of name was that? Especially since the guy had a beaky nose and a scrawny figure under the voluminous swaddle of his coat. Maybe it was a joke. Maybe the idea was to make people think he was something he wasn't.

And that's when Sally knew exactly what to do.

As the man stepped forward, she threw herself to her knees with a wail loud enough to wake the dead. Luckily, that didn't happen. She shuffled forward a few feet on her knees, wrapping her arms around Fat Lorenzo's legs.

"Please don't hurt us, mister," she begged, and then she bit down on her tongue hard enough to draw blood. Tears rushed to her eyes, and she tilted her head back so the moon would shine on them. Fat Lorenzo didn't drop his gun and apologize, but she hadn't expected that. No, she lived with brothers, and she knew that this kind of behavior wasn't going to miraculously make him buy her penny candy. But it would make him underestimate her, and that was the advantage she needed.

"Get off me, kid!" he exclaimed, shoving at her with one arm.

She held on tight, crying and begging, and no matter how hard he tried to dislodge her, she refused to let go.

Finally, he looked up to James, who stood frozen and awaiting the outcome.

Fat Lorenzo threw up his arms in exasperation and snarled at her brother. "Get her—"

Sally wasn't sure what the end of the sentence would have been. He never got to finish it. As soon as his attention was off her, she clutched the wrench that had been concealed by the long folds of her robe. It swung in a long, glittering arc. She screamed ferociously as metal met flesh with a bone-splitting crack. The gun went flying into the pricker bush, and Fat Lorenzo shrieked in pain.

"My hand!" he yelled, falling to his knees and clutching it. "My hand! I'll get you, you..."

Sally didn't wait to hear the end of that sentence, either. She turned, holding the wrench in front of her like a sword at the ready. She must have had her war face on—Jet had commented a few times on how scary it was—because James reflexively held his hands up, dropping the control device. She swept it up off the ground and ran.

"Come on!" she urged him. He didn't need much urging. Together they fled down the path toward the house.

CHAPTER 7

Branches whipped at her face and crackled under her feet. Between the two of them, she and James were louder than a herd of stampeding cattle. She knew it would be smart to go to ground, but she couldn't resist the urge to get as far away from the gun as possible. Sally heard shouting behind them, and deep, angry voices answering. She knew without being told that Fat Lorenzo had friends, and they were not happy about the fact that she'd shattered his hand and made off with the controller. She tucked it into her pocket, pausing on the path.

"We can't...lead them to the house," James gasped, doubled over.

The sharp *bang bang* of a gun underscored his words. Sally ducked reflexively, but the noise was far behind them down the path. What were they shooting at, and would the noise attract the rest of her family? If Fat Lorenzo threatened her Ma, Sally was going to make him pay somehow. Some things just weren't done, and holding a gun on a lady with a baby was one of them.

"We split up," she said decisively, trying to keep her voice down. James gave her a skeptical glance and opened his mouth to argue, but she overrode him. "Lead them through the potatoes to Thresher Field. I'll get the rest of the boys up. They can bring their snares."

After a moment, his eyes lit with recognition.

"Good plan." It was slim praise but all she was likely to get. He chucked her on the chin before breaking a wide path through the bracken off to the right of the path.

"Drop something," she said. "They're city boys. I bet their wood-craft is really bad, so you're gonna have to advertise."

James grinned and let his pocket handkerchief fall to the ground, marking the trail as effectively as a street sign. Then, with a sketchy salute, he backed into the darkness.

"If we don't catch up before then, I'll meet you at the blind," he said, and then he began a crashing descent into the woods. "Come on, city boys!" he yelled gleefully. "Come get me!"

Fat Lorenzo's cronies shouted in response.

"This way, fellas!"

"We're gonna shut your mouth for you, pretty boy!"

There was no time to waste, but now wasn't the time for panicked flight. Sally dropped to her knees, groping along the soft ground beside the trail. It hadn't rained much lately, but the sun didn't reach this deep into the woods, and there was plenty of mud for her to roll around in. She stood back up, the glow of her white nightgown muddled by clumps of dirt and leaves. Ma was going to throw a fit, but it was a fit worth enduring if it meant that the mysterious mobsters wouldn't spot her through the trees and shoot her.

Thus disguised, she crept up the path on the balls of her feet. She'd been hunting with Pa before and had gotten pretty good at scouting ahead for prey. If she needed to move silently, she could, and this was one time when the skill came in awful handy.

The sounds of pursuit grew distant behind her, and she knew the bad guys had taken the bait. But that didn't mean she could get cocky.

That was the kind of attitude likely to get her killed. She made her way deliberately to the house, trying not to giggle at the thought of James leading his pursuers through Thresher Field, where old and busted farm equipment went to die. She'd gotten a lot of Calamity's parts from that field, but there was plenty of sharp metal still left for the bad guys to trip on. Some of the stuff had been there so long that the grass had grown up over it. There was no way to know it was there until you were on top of it. But the Slick kids knew. They'd spent weeks running obstacle courses through there, until Henry had tripped and cut his hand on a twisted piece of metal. It had gotten infected, and that was the end of that game.

With luck, all of the bad guys would get so injured they'd have to give up the chase, but Sally wasn't willing to make that bet. She needed a Plan B, and her brothers were an important part of it. She charged into the house, trying to move with equal parts speed and silence, and ran straight into Ma with the baby over her shoulder.

"Sally Mae Slick," she said, her words muffled by a long yawn. "What are you doing all over mud in the middle of the night?"

"I was..." Sally looked around wildly for an excuse. She couldn't tell Ma about the men with the guns. Pa hadn't come back from the cattle auction yet. Ma couldn't go out to confront those men with the baby. Besides, she and James could handle this, right? Fat Lorenzo hadn't shot her because he was just bluffing. She knew it. Now that she had a chance to catch her breath, she found to her surprise that she was kind of enjoying herself. Telling her mother would only end the fun.

"I was sleepwalking," she said firmly. She'd never done it, but Isaiah sometimes did. You'd find him in the middle of the yard in the morning with an empty pot and no idea what he was doing out there.

It was a testament to Ma's exhaustion that she didn't even question the excuse. "Go back to bed," she said, and then she turned around to walk up the stairs. This would have worked a lot better if she'd been standing two feet to the left. As it stood, she went face first into the wall. Ralphie stirred in her arms, and both of them froze, terrified of waking him up.

"Let me help, Ma," Sally said. The easiest way to make sure they were both out of harm's way was to put them there. And given how sleep-deprived Ma obviously was, Sally wasn't entirely certain she'd make it to her bed without falling over.

"You're a good girl, Sally. A little wild, but I was too..." Ma allowed Sally to take the baby; he snorted and settled into the crook of her arm. He barely weighed anything. It felt like a stiff breeze might blow him away. She wasn't the kind of girl who got all gushy over babies—how could you when all they did was sleep and poo and throw up all over everything? But she felt a fierce wave of protectiveness as she looked down at his smushed little face. He might be an annoyance, but he was *her* annoyance, and no gangster with a gun was going to touch a hair on his head.

She settled him into his bassinet and pulled the blanket over him. Ma rolled into bed and began snoring within seconds. It was all too easy to creep back out the door, down the hall, and into the twins' room.

Two steps inside, her foot hit a roller skate and slid right out from underneath her. She found herself doing the splits between the beds, and then there was an arm around her neck.

"State yer business," hissed Henry. Either he was having a pirate dream or...no, she couldn't come up with any other reason why he should be talking with that ridiculous accent.

"Let go!" she whispered. "I can't breathe."

His grip loosened but didn't release entirely. It took some dedicated wriggling and a carefully placed pinch before she was free.

"What is it?" Isaiah sat up, taking his glasses from the bedside table and putting them on upside down. It was a measure of how distracted Sally really was that she didn't take the opportunity to make fun of him for that.

"James is in trouble," she said, and that got their attention right quick. Henry quit squinting at her and sat bolt upright, and Isaiah resettled his glasses and began slipping on his socks. "Some men from the city followed him here. They have guns."

"Is he okay?" Henry's voice came out cold and completely lacking his usual singsong.

"He was when I left him. They weren't shooting at us, just trying to spook us, I think." Both boys relaxed visibly at this, and she tried to look reassuring. "He's leading them to Thresher Field."

Henry looked down at the long scar looping along the edge of his palm and snorted. "Nice."

"But it won't keep them busy for long. Come quick. And bring your snares. If we can annoy them enough, they'll give up and go home."

Henry blinked at her, but Isaiah leapt into action. He stood, shrugging into his robe, and pushed his glasses up onto his nose with his thumb.

"Henry, get everyone up. I'll map out the territory." He grabbed a pencil and a sheet of paper and began furiously scribbling. Sally craned over his shoulder, pointing.

"Don't forget the workshop," she suggested.

"I won't. Now hush so I can concentrate." The words weren't unkind, and it wasn't going to help anything to pick a fight, so Sally let them slide. She sat quietly while each of her brothers came in, got a quick rundown of the problem, and made hasty whispered plans to set up their hunting snares in a particular location. Pretty soon, all of them were gone except Isaiah, Sally, and Carl. That was strange, because Carl was the best hunter of them all. Sally would have sent him out first and foremost.

"You have your rifle?" Isaiah asked quietly. He looked older somehow than he had that morning.

Carl nodded shortly. "Yup."

"Guard the house."

"But..." Sally couldn't keep from interrupting. "Didn't you hear me before? They aren't going to shoot. Fat Lorenzo could have shot us, but he didn't. They're just trying to scare us."

"You want to bet Ma and Ralphie's life on that?" asked Isaiah. "If they're not serious, this plan should send them packing. But it could also make them mad. I'm not leaving this house until I know Ma's safe."

Carl clapped him on the shoulder. "You can count on me. Go order the troops, Field Marshall."

Isaiah stuck his tongue out and became the 15-year-old Sally recognized once more. Which was good, because if he'd been abducted by aliens, she wasn't sure how she'd handle it.

"What about me?" she asked. "You can't just leave me out of the plan. Not again."

"You need to put that big mouth of yours to good use." He grinned and thrust the map toward her. "James won't know where the traps are. You'll have to find him and keep him from killing his fool self."

"Done and done."

She snatched the map, crept down the stairs, and went right out the door before Ma could wake up and stop her again. The maple at the corner of the porch rustled, and she nearly threw the wrench up into its branches before she realized it was Carl taking his position. Now that she saw him there, settling his rifle onto his lap and angling for the best vantage point of the front and back yards, she realized it did make her feel better to know he was there. She could take the fight to the bad guys without worrying they were flanking her.

It felt just like a real military maneuver. Jet would have flipped. He was crazy about that kind of thing.

She flashed Carl a thumbs up and began running. Isaiah was at her heels, but before long they split up, and she was alone. Crab grass thrashed her bare ankles, and once she barked her toes on a rock and nearly fell right over, but she kept going. It felt like they'd wasted too much time talking, and now that she was out here in the dark, she realized that maybe this situation was more serious than she'd treated it. Even if those men didn't shoot her brother, there were other things they could do. Bad things. And the fact that they'd followed him all the way from Chicago suggested that they were serious even if they weren't aiming at them when they pulled the trigger.

She ran faster—Thresher Field was at the edge of their property so it was a long trip. By the time she crested the hill and approached her destination, she was huffing. Her breath came so loud and so fast that she didn't hear the man until a moment before they collided.

He was stocky with a wispy mustache that looked like it was an inch away from wilting right off his face. She instantly knew he was a stranger and therefore the enemy, partly because she was acquainted with everyone who lived nearby, but also because he was wearing what she was beginning to think of as the Standard Bad Guy Uniform: black trench coat, starched white shirt, black trousers, and a bowler.

They hit hard enough to send them both flying. Sally toppled over, went into a smooth somersault without quite understanding how she'd done it, and kept on going. The success of their plan depended on speed, and if she allowed herself to be detained, it would all be over.

Without even looking back, she knew he was tailing her. That could be because he yelled, "Hey, kid! Stop! Stop or I'll shoot!" But he didn't shoot, and she refused to believe he'd do such a thing. She kept on going.

Then she heard a loud bang, and the ground exploded about twenty feet to her left. Clods of dirt flew everywhere.

Apparently, she'd been wrong about the whole gun thing. It seemed like she should be panicking, but the whole thing felt so unreal. Like it was happening to someone else. And really, she didn't have any time to sit down and reflect on her feelings. She veered abruptly to the right, hoping against hope that her brothers had been able to set the tripwire in their usual spot along the deer run but she couldn't slow down enough to tell. She flew into a stand of goldenrod, which sent up spurts of yellow fluff to mark her passage. She'd always found it pretty, but today, it was more than that. Today, it was camouflage.

A piff and a bang signaled another shot. Her heart pounded, and she knew if she stopped, she'd roll up into a ball and never come up again. But she couldn't. If the situation with Jet and Eugene had taught her anything, it's that hiding your head in the sand like an ostrich didn't do anything to fix the problem. And you ended up with sand up your nose.

She veered again into the trees and down the run where she and her brothers had nabbed seven rabbits before the bunnies got wise to their snares. But she was willing to bet that these city slickers had no idea what a snare was.

The trees were in sight. Two sturdy trunks closely abutted the narrow trail, a deep patch of leaves between them. Rubble bordered the twisty path along both sides, making navigation even more difficult. She reached it and leaped, trying not to make it too obvious but not really knowing how to leap casually. The pounding footsteps of pursuit faltered as the man realized something was up and maybe he should do something about it, but by then it was too late. His foot caught the tripwire, and he went down hard into the rocks. He let out a yelp of pain as his cheekbone struck the pointed edge of a stone. She quit looking back after that.

One man down, but she was winded, and were a few tripwires really going to send these men packing? They'd shot at her. With a real gun and everything. She began to think the Slicks were hopelessly out-numbered. But town was a couple of miles away, and their house was on a rural telephone line that shut down late at night. The only way to get the police was to run all the way to town, and by the time she got there, it would all be over. Her brothers were counting on her. She couldn't bug out.

She had to bring something else. Something that would scare the men enough. Something that would make them run.

A slow grin spread across her dirty face. She knew exactly what to do.

CHAPTER 8

The racing tractor burst through the workshop doors with a belch of exhaust. Sally had dampened the engines with a makeshift rig, so there was no satisfying roar of power, but that was okay. The bad guys wouldn't hear her until she was right on top of them. She'd be the surprise tractor cavalry coming to the rescue.

The tractor ate up the ground, quickly accelerating until it was going faster than most motor cars Sally'd been in. Calamity was a galloping horse made of steel and iron, and she was going to take those men down. Sally barely restrained herself from whooping aloud as she crested the hill for the umpteenth time that night.

Perched atop the tractor's high seat and no longer puffing for air, she had a much better view of the situation now than she'd had before. None of her brothers were visible, but they weren't supposed to be so she tried not to worry about that. She saw more Standard Bad Guy bowler hats than she could count, most of them in small packs that roamed like wolves over the fields. She couldn't see their bodies, obscured as they were by the green of growing things, but she assumed the hats were attached to bad guys. And bad guys could be run down, if one had a racing tractor at one's disposal.

There. A pair of bad guys off by themselves in the weeds to the left. They were separated from the herd like deer. The perfect prey. As she swung in their direction, one of them disappeared. Caught by a snare, probably. His partner whirled around, his gun drawn. If she was going to intervene, now was the time. Sally smiled a shark-like grin and pressed the red button on Calamity's dashboard, the one she'd never pressed, the one she'd saved for the unwinnable race.

It was a button that would work in theory, hopefully without blowing her up in the process. With that much pressure behind the pistons, there was a definite chance that it might.

But the booster worked. The motor responded with an instant surge of speed that threw her back in her seat, springs jouncing her around wildly. The noise of the engine grew to a low, teeth-rattling hum. And then, strangely, it lurched again, clunked once, and slowed back down. She risked a frantic glance back at the booster engine, and that glance told her all she needed to know. Wispy curls of smoke wafted from it. Not enough coolant; she should have gone air cooled instead of water cooled after all. If she'd had time, she would have kicked herself.

Without the booster, was Calamity fast enough? She was faster than a regular tractor, but without the surge of speed from the booster, could this plan work? Despite her best efforts, she couldn't come up with another one. This had to work.

"Come out, kid!" shouted the man on the path in front of her. Initially Sally thought he was talking to her, but was he really? He had to have heard the engine, but he hadn't even turned around to look at her. Even though she wasn't gaining on him as fast as she had been with the booster, he had to know she was still close enough to be a threat.

James stepped out into the open with his arms held up high. His hands were visibly shaking as the man held the gun on him, stepping closer to shove it right into his nose. She buried the pedal. The man in the bowler hat paused, his head swiveling as he finally decided to look for the source of the noise. She'd show him. She'd show him firsthand.

"Banzai!" she shouted, unable to restrain herself. "Eat tractor!"

The gun whirled in her direction, and the man fired off a wild shot that pinged off the fuselage. Sally knew she should duck. Ducking would be wise, but she found herself hunched over the wheel like Mr. Toad during his wild ride, laughing maniacally. The man looked up at her and, more to the point, at the tons of metal moments away from smushing him into goo, and threw himself off to one side.

She couldn't have planned things better. The man with the gun threw himself into the spot where the Vampire Thresher awaited, half sunken into the ground. Rusty, pointy bits of metal stuck randomly out of the dirt, waiting for blood to suck. The thresher was infamous. She'd fallen on it once during one of her adventures with Jet, and she still had scars dotting her legs. Few people who tangled with it escaped unscathed.

Time hadn't dulled the metal. The man began to shriek at the top of his lungs, and she almost felt bad enough to stop and check on him. But not quite.

Instead, she took the dampener off the engine, loosening the clip and letting the pad fall to the ground. Normally, she wouldn't just toss away equipment moments after inventing it, but now wasn't a good time to piffle around in the weeds looking for it. The engine responded with a satisfactory roar, and the combination of wild screams and ominous rumble was more effective than the snares had been. She could hear the men yelling in the fields, urging each other to flee from the unheard beast in the underbrush.

"Help me!" yelled the man who had fallen onto the Vampire Thresher. "Oh god, it's got my leg!"

She couldn't keep from giggling a little as she slowed down slightly to pick up James. A few yards ahead of her, another man burst through the trees.

"Joey Two-Fist?" he yelled, too intent on finding his comrade to notice her for the moment. "Where are you?"

"Down here!"

The man moved two steps forward, but then, as James swung himself up onto Calamity's running board, the motion seemed to catch his eye. He stopped and whirled around to face them. One moment, his hand was empty. The next, it clutched a wicked looking knife. The man was imposing enough without the knife—he had the kind of sturdy, muscular build that made you want to be on his good side—but with it, he was positively frightening. A long scar bisected his cheek and tugged at his lip. His eyes were like ice, cold and keen. They evaluated the tractor, its driver, and its passenger, and then flicked down to the weapon in his hand. His body relaxed, and he put the knife away.

That confused Sally more than anything else. "Aren't you going to attack us?" she asked.

"My odds aren't so good, miss," he replied, as casual as you please. "Think we could reach an arrangement? I'll take my man off your hands, and we'll agree to not try and kill each other?"

"And that's it? You shoot at us, and then you expect me to let you go, as nice as you please?"

"*I* didn't shoot at you. I don't shoot kids."

"Well, he did." She gestured toward the one still entangled on the Vampire Thresher.

The scarred man's eyes narrowed, and Sally felt chills run along her arms. From the looks of things, she didn't want to be the one making this man angry. Not one bit.

"I'll make sure it doesn't happen again. You have my word."

"Don't listen to him, Sally." James elbowed her in the side. "He's a crook. The Steel Syndicate is infamous for making promises they don't keep, and he's one of their higher ups."

She didn't even stop to consider it. Regardless of what her brother said, she'd learned to trust her instincts, and they were telling her that this so-called crook was a man of his word. "Go ahead," she urged the man. "Get him and get out."

"Thanks, missy." He tipped his hat.

James gave a disgusted snort and threw his hands up. She expected him to complain, but instead he just glared at them both. Sally thought it was a fine way to treat the girl who had just saved your life, but what did she know?

The man with the scarred face made his way carefully down through the pieces of the Vampire Thresher and picked up his writhing comrade in an over-the-shoulder carry. The injured man's pants were ripped and dotted with red marks where the thresher had...well, *threshed* him. His face was red, and blood vessels bulged from his neck as he continued to shout.

"It's stuck in my leg!" he yelled. "My leg!"

"Shut up, you bimbo," snarled the scarred man. Thankfully, it worked.

The scarred man stopped on the path, eyeing Sally atop the tractor, and James standing at her side. He seemed to realize that he was giving way to a teenage girl, and his eyes darted quickly around as he evaluated the situation. Sally knew that the tractor wouldn't provide any protection against a gun, and she couldn't let him come to that conclusion, too. So she fiddled with the clutch and tried to look like she was ready to fire a mysterious weapon from the depths of her tractor.

If she made it out of this alive, she'd have to add one.

Maybe he bought it or maybe not. Either way, he took a moment to tip his hat one more time to her before he left.

"Miss," he said. "Well played."

"Don't come back," she said. But something made her add a single word. "Please."

"We'll see," he replied noncommittally. And then he turned, adjusting his burden on his back, and trudged away.

CHAPTER 9

"It's broken," Sally wailed. She was tired and dirty and sore, and she could have handled all of those things. But seeing BEM's mangled torso pushed her over the edge. She dropped to her knees, letting the now-useless control device fall into the dirt. A tear plopped down next to it, and she swiped the back of her hand angrily across her cheek.

But for once, her brothers didn't make fun of her for being a weak little girl. Isaiah patted her shoulder awkwardly, and Henry shifted from foot to foot.

"You could fix it..." John suggested tentatively.

"Yeah," added Henry. "You built that tractor from scratch, Sal. If anyone could do it, you could."

She frowned. It was nice of them to suggest, but she didn't even know where to begin. A machine this complicated wasn't something you could just toss together like chicken and biscuits. And everyone knew how well *that* had turned out.

"James?" She licked her lips nervously. Her hands moved restlessly, wanting to touch the smooth metal of the robot like it might communicate to her somehow and tell her what to do. Because wasn't that how she made things? She listened to the metal talking, and wasn't that just winging it? She wasn't trained. She hadn't apprenticed under anyone. She was just a farm girl and not old enough to take on a project like this. "No," she said, shaking her head. "This is too much. I'm sorry, but I can't do this. I couldn't even make a booster engine for Calamity that didn't slag itself in the first 30 seconds." She hung her head in shame, her eyes still leaking.

"I think you can." James ran his hand through his hair. "I know I should have come to you first, but I was worried you'd think..."

"That you're a robot thief?" She laughed a little through her tears. "I wonder why."

Henry grinned, elbowing James. "She got you there, brother."

"Shut up," James replied reflexively, and the Slick boys all relaxed. They were back into familiar argumentative territory now. And no one was shooting at them, which was a nice added bonus.

Maybe if James of all people believed in her, she really could do this. And whether she could or not, she realized she desperately wanted to try.

"You do realize that this could go badly, right? I could end up destroying it, and there won't be any going back," said Sally.

James toed the twisted metal at his feet. "At this point, I don't think we can go anywhere but up."

"Thanks for the vote of confidence," she said dryly, and Isaiah laughed. "All right. Help me get it into the workshop. We'll hide it in my spare parts pile, and I'll work on it after school."

"Yes, mawster," drawled Henry. He laughed at his own joke until she slugged him one in the stomach, and then things really dissolved into chaos.

It was hard to return to school the next day. Sally felt like she'd just gone to sleep when Ma shook her awake. It took three more shakes and a threatening bucket of cold water fresh from the pump before she actually managed to get up. She washed up at the bucket in the hopes that the chill would help, and it did leave her feeling alert enough as she dressed and plaited her hair into braids. It wore off quickly, though. She fell asleep at the table and went face first into her oatmeal.

By the time she managed to wash the oats out of her ears, she was late, and Miss Cranston had promised dire punishments if she was tardy again. She sprinted down the driveway without her satchel, ran back to get it, then had to go back a second time for her lunch, and...well, by that time the conclusion was inevitable. She spent the morning in the corner and stayed after the last bell to write an essay on *Why Punctuality Is Important*. It was very tempting to say that she felt punctuality was important if one wanted to avoid having to write stupid essays, but she'd tried a stunt like that before, and it hadn't ended well. She still squirmed every time she thought of the look on Miss Cranston's face when she'd read it. But then again, Miss Cranston didn't have a sense of humor, and it was rumored that the only time she'd ever smiled was when someone had died. That seemed a little over the top, but Sally had to admit that she'd lost ten rolls of candy buttons after betting that she could coax a smile out of the old biddy. Maybe if she'd faked her own death, it might have worked.

She began musing over how to fake said death as she descended the steps outside the schoolhouse. From inside, Miss Cranston yelled, "Close the door, Sally! Were you born in a barn?"

"Yes," she murmured, but not too loud because the woman had ears like a hawk. "As a matter of fact, I was. So there."

The exchange made her a little irritable. The whole thing where city folk put on airs like they were better than you just because you lived on a farm and wore your brothers' hand-me-downs really got her goat. Except the Slick family didn't keep goats any more.

Anyway, Jet usually waited for her when she was kept after school. It was the kind of thing that happened often enough to require a plan of attack, since neither of them really liked walking home alone. Sally thought it was boring, and Jet was well versed in the use of the buddy system to avoid getting pummeled. He really could have used the backup today, because when Sally cut across the grass and turned the corner, she found him up against the brick wall of the school with Eugene Falks's hands at his throat.

Sally froze for a moment. She'd expected retaliation, sure. She wasn't stupid, and boys like Eugene don't just let things slide. If he didn't make an example of her and Jet, he'd lose all his power and people would realize he was just a big dumb lug with fists like hams, and why were they afraid of *that*? Especially when you stopped to consider that a ham was just a big old pig butt.

Unfortunately for Jet, one pig butt was currently raising into the air, preparing to smash into his face.

The odds weren't good. It was just her and Jet—who could tell a killer adventure story but had only thrown one punch in his life and broke his own hand in the process—against Eugene and the two members of his gang, Fred and Christopher. She'd have to even up those odds and hope for the best. It seemed like suicide, but she'd meant it when she vowed to quit letting these things slide.

She had her primer and slate slung on a book strap by her side. There was no time to lose. As Eugene's fist began its descent toward Jet, she whipped the book overhead with a quick flick of the wrist and then released it. The book flew through the air, followed by the hurtling figure of Sally Slick, fists clenched and ready to go.

The book whomped the side of Fred's head, and his face went from amused leer to pained leer in about two seconds flat. He clapped a hand to his ear and howled. Sally bowled him right over, aiming for Eugene. She would have gone through Christopher too, but he was ready for her. He grabbed her by the back of the dress, ripping the lace collar Ma had so painstakingly sewed on, and that only made Sally madder than a coon in a trap. She kicked and flailed wildly, screeching at the top of her lungs.

"You let him go! Rat faced cowards!" she yelled. "Can't even handle a fair fight, can you?"

"Shut up, Slick," Eugene snarled. "Why won't you just shut up and go knit something? It's like you think you're a boy."

"What's it to you if I do?" she said, struggling in vain.

His face went red, and finally she realized what bothered him so much about her. He never picked on the other girls, but Sally was a threat. And Jet continued to stand up to the Falks Gang. Maybe he kept getting beaten up for his trouble, but he never backed down like the other kids. Eugene didn't pick on them because they were weak. He did it because they were a threat.

The thought made her feel tremendously brave. "Poor baby," she taunted, tearing free of Christopher. "You're scared of a kid who's half your size, aren't you?"

She would have said more, except that Christopher slugged her in the stomach. All the air went out of her, and she fell to her knees in the dirt. Her head swam, less from the blow and more from all this anger building up inside her. What good was it to see that things were wrong if you couldn't do anything about it? She wanted to make an army of metal men and send them out against the Eugene Falks of the world.

"I would have let him off easy," said Eugene, pushing Jet against the wall where he sniffled and swatted weakly at his attacker. "But you just had to shove your nose in, didn't you? Now I've got to make an example of him, and it's all your fault."

"Jeez," Sally muttered into the dirt, trying to ignore the pain in her belly. "All you need to do now is dry-wash your hands, and you'll sound like every adventure villain ever created. Sad thing is, you'll never be anything but a no-account schoolyard bully."

He kicked her in the ribs, and this time it felt like all the air went out of the *world*. The edges of her vision went white. She clutched her side and rolled around on the ground, waiting for the next blow. Only it never came.

"That's enough."

The voice was deep and unexpected, and it came from the opposite side of the chain link fence that bordered the school grounds. Sally squinted in that direction from her spot in the dirt, but her eyes couldn't focus through the tears swimming in them. All she could see was a black shirt topped with a fedora and a blurry, pale face. But the voice...that voice was familiar somehow.

"We're just playing around, mister." Eugene's voice took on that aw-shucks tone he used whenever adults were around. "Adventure tales and all that. I'm the sinister man in black, and I'm trying to get them to give me the location of the buried treasure. Aren't I, guys?"

He elbowed Jet, and Sally knew how this would go. Jet would cave, the way he always had, and the man would leave, and then Eugene would beat them both up. She loved Jet. Really she did, but it was time for him stand up for *himself* for once. Didn't he see that? He'd intervene on someone else's behalf without an eyelash flutter, but getting him to defend himself was like trying to design an engine that ran on tapioca. It wasn't ever going to happen.

Her frustration must have shown on her face, or maybe Jet had just had enough. Because he didn't go along with Eugene's lie. For the first time in his life, he said, "No."

It was like time had stopped. No one quite knew what to do.

"What—what do you mean, 'No'?" Eugene asked, his jocular voice slipping slightly to reveal the anger underneath.

"I'm not letting you beat on Sally." Jet's voice grew in power as he continued. "That's wrong! You shouldn't hit girls! I'm...I'm sick of you, Eugene Falks! I've had enough!"

"Here, kid," said the mystery man in the black suit. He ambled up all casual-like, as if this kind of schoolyard confrontation was nothing special. Maybe it wasn't to him, but to Sally it felt like the whole of their future hung on this moment. Either they would be pond scum for the rest of their lives, waiting for bullies like Eugene to pick them off, or they'd become something bigger than that. "Use this."

He handed Jet something long and metal that sparkled in the sunlight. Sally's eyes were still watery, and her vantage point wasn't the best, but even she could tell that it wasn't going to make much of a weapon. It looked like a very flimsy rapier. The blade was so thin that it actually wobbled.

Sadly, Jet didn't share her skepticism. He was big into duels—most of the adventures of Calamity Sue and Jet Blackwood had involved Jet picking up a stick and dueling with someone, usually to the death and often over a pit or some other deadly obstacle. So getting a rapier and permission to use it in real life was a dream come true for him. His eyes lit up as he raised the weapon in a grand salute that would have been very impressive if he'd been about a foot taller, fifty pounds heavier, and wearing a costume with a cape. As it was, no one took him particularly seriously until he extended in a perfect lunge, pressing the tip of the rapier into Eugene's chest. The metal bent; there was the unmistakable hum and crackle of electrical discharge. And then, Eugene fell into a limp pile on the ground, moaning weakly.

"Uh…" Christopher began to back away, exchanging a look with Fred.

"We should…um…go," added Fred.

The two of them didn't even have the decency to look back as they ran for it. Sally thought about chasing them, even entertained a nice mini daydream about holding them down while Jet whacked them on the head with the rapier, but she settled for a vain attempt to try to clean the scrapes on her elbows with the hem of her shirt.

"Hrm," said the man. She recognized him now. He was the one with the scar on his face from last night, the one who hadn't seemed afraid of her. He was certainly the enemy, so why was he helping them? Was it just to lure them into complacency so he could betray them later? She found that she really didn't care, because Eugene Falks was on the ground, and he was drooling, and that was awesome.

"You'd better hit the chap again." The man pulled out a fancy cigarette case and placed one between his lips, spitting the words out of the other side of his mouth. "The results on this thing are still a little wild."

"Sally?" Jet's eyes were bright with triumph, but he still looked to her for confirmation.

She wanted to see what would happen. What was that electric discharge for? Where had it come from? Now that she was looking for it, she could see circuitry at the base of the rapier, and she wanted to see it in action when she wasn't so busy gasping for oxygen.

"Go on," she urged.

It was all the permission he needed. He raised the rapier to the salute again and tapped Eugene with it. This time, Sally swore she could see the charge travel up the blade and onto Eugene, where it spread over his entire body. But what did it do?

Eugene sat up and quacked like a duck.

"Quack." He blinked, his eyes going buggy as he attempted to look at his own mouth without a mirror. He seemed panicked and unable to stop making duck noises, which was pretty funny. "Quack quack! Quackquackquack QUACKquack!"

Sally couldn't resist it any longer. She pushed up to her feet and snatched the weapon from Jet's unresisting hand. He was too busy staring at Eugene and trying not to laugh.

"He's a duck, Sal! Eugene Falks thinks he's a duck!" Jet slapped his leg and began guffawing like this was the funniest thing ever.

"I know," she replied without even looking up from the rapier. "Can't he say anything other than 'quack'? Because it's getting annoying already."

"QUACK!"

"Shut up," she said.

Sadly, there were no labels on the rapier that told her exactly what it was, and all of her tools were in her workshop so she couldn't just dive into the circuitry and figure it out herself. The current clearly was designed to affect the target, but how?

"Well?" The man cupped his hand around his cigarette, trying to shield it from the wind as he lit up. "What do you think, lassie?"

"Don't call me 'lassie,'" Sally replied automatically. "What is it?"

"Neural Stimulator." He exhaled a long plume of smoke that made her cough. "You can keep it if you want."

"Why would I want to do that?" she asked cautiously.

"Peace offering."

"QUACK!"

"Shut up!" All three of them said it this time, and then they grinned at each other.

"So it...stimulates his brain?" she asked thoughtfully.

"That's how the doc explained it to me, yeah, but I ain't the science type so I can't tell you a whole lot more. It's fun to use, but the effects are completely random. It'll make a man blind one time, and then the next, it'll turn him paranoid or cut out the use of his legs. Nifty little gadget, but it's impossible to anticipate what'll happen when you use it."

"Probably because it's such an indirect connection..." added Sally.

"I can't say you're wrong, missy. The doc says we can exert more control if we wire it straight into a fella's melon." The man shuddered. "I'd rather not."

"So you're just going to give it to a couple of kids," joked Jet.

"Nah. I'm giving it to *her*."

Jet's face fell until Sally said, "It's okay, Jet. You're a better swordsman than I am, anyway. You keep it. Just let me take it apart later."

"If that's okay...?" Jet eyed the man nervously.

"Fine by me. It's not so useful for combat situations. You never know if your opponent is going to fall over limp or start in on his best duck impression while he beats you into a pulp."

"QUACK!" Eugene flailed around, flapping his arms like wings.

"Will it wear off?" asked Jet, eyeing the bully with satisfaction.

"Yeah, he'll get better eventually. And he'd better have learned his lesson about messing with the two of you, eh?" The scarred man glared down at Eugene, who waddled hastily out of striking range with wide, frightened eyes. Sally snickered despite herself.

"Let me drive you two home. I got my motorcar right over here on the lane." The man started across the yard without even bothering to see if they'd follow him.

"I'm not sure that's..." Jet didn't get to finish his sentence, because Sally grabbed her books from the ground and scrambled to catch up, leaving Eugene quacking angrily in the dust. "Wait up!"

She may have been eager to hear more about the amazing inventions that were suddenly popping up all over the place, but Sally wasn't stupid. She walked up to the long, black, sleek motorcar and looked at the man holding the door open. The scar bisecting his cheek pulled at his lip, giving him a faint smile even when his face was set and serious as it was now. It made her like him a little despite herself.

"Wait a minute," she said, trying to ignore the lure of the leather and metal of the car. She'd never been in one this nice before. "Why are you being so kind to us?"

He tipped his hat to her. "Because, Miss Slick. I think I forgot to introduce myself. The name's Frankie Ratchet, and I'm second in command to the Steel Don of Chicago. I'm here to offer you a job."

CHAPTER 10

Sally bent to enter the rich smelling interior of the motorcar with a barely suppressed giggle. Whoever heard of adults wanting to hire a fourteen-year-old girl for a real job? Working on a farm, sure. She knew of a couple of kids who had left school early to work in factories or farms. Her parents talked a lot about how lucky the Slick kids were to go to school, because in their day, kids had to work all day long, and they didn't have shoes, and they had to walk there uphill both ways, and...

It was all a crock, but you had to listen anyway.

But the idea that this man in his fancy suit would want to hire someone like her was a good joke.

"Nice one, mister," she said, scooting over so Jet could fit on the seat beside her.

"Not a joke, missy."

The man tipped his hat to her before shutting the door on them. Now that the thrill of victory was beginning to wane, Sally began to realize that this wasn't the best of ideas. She and Jet were getting into a motorcar with a strange man who worked for someone named the Steel Don. She'd read enough adventure tales to know that a man like that wasn't the kind of person you trifled with. He usually had goons at his disposal, and they liked to tie heroes up and suspend them over pits full of boiling acid or hungry piranha. They were not the kind of people you went for joyrides in motorcars with.

"Get out, Jet," she hissed, and he looked at her blankly, running his hand over the dashboard.

"Look how shiny...wait. What?" he said.

But it was too late. Frankie Ratchet sat down on the smooth leather seat next to her. His thigh pressed up against hers, and she scooted as close to Jet as she could to escape the contact. Mr. Ratchet didn't seem to notice. He started the motorcar, and it took off with a purr and a rumble. It was fast, too. The kind of fast that makes you rethink your plan to jump out and make a run for it.

"What do you think?" asked Mr. Ratchet.

"Um...about what?" Sally tried to sound confident, but her voice wouldn't stop shaking.

He arched a brow at her. The scar on his face puckered. She tried not to stare and failed.

"The job offer," he repeated deliberately. "We'd like you to work for the Steel Syndicate. What do you think?"

"I think you're pulling my leg, Mr. Ratchet," she said. She tried to sound polite, but in the meantime she was counting the seconds until they reached the crossroads. He would have to stop. It would be the prime opportunity to get out of the car; she just had to figure out a way to communicate the plan to Jet.

"I'm perfectly serious. Your brother told us all about you. You're just the kind of girl we need designing machines for us. I'm authorized to make a very generous offer."

"Was that before or after your goons pulled guns on us?"

Her mouth rattled off the question before she had a chance to evaluate whether or not it was wise to ask. Jet made a noise something like *eep* and pinched her, but it was too late. But Frankie Ratchet just laughed. It sounded like whiskey over gravel. Sally had snuck a sip of whiskey once on a dare from John. Some days, it felt like her throat was still on fire.

"Before," he said. "My instructions were to secure the return of the BEM Model 1 robot and recruit you to join us. I would have preferred to ask first and pull the gun second, but I didn't find you fast enough. Some of the employees of the Steel Syndicate don't share my morals, more's the pity."

"Well, thanks but no thanks," she said tartly. "You seem nice enough, and I'm flattered and all, but I don't think I could work with the kind of people who try to shoot kids."

"We could remove them."

The offer came with such casualness that it made her shudder. Maybe "remove" meant that he'd have them fired. Maybe it was a perfectly innocent thing. But somehow, she was certain that he was talking about something much more permanent. Something that may or may not involve the application of cement shoes...

The car slowed as Frankie Ratchet made a right turn at the crossroads without bothering to stop. They had to get out of the car. Sally threw open the door and shoved Jet out into thin air before he could so much as peep. Or quack.

In midair, Sally had what felt like an eternity to think about what a bad idea this was and how much it was going to hurt when they landed. But then Jet grabbed her around the waist, twisted, and rolled. They hit the dirt with much less bone-jarring force than she expected, and Jet even managed to roll right back up to his feet. She stared at him with blank shock. She would have asked him how he'd managed it, but she heard the rumble of gravel behind them as the car began to roll to a stop.

"We've got to get out of here," she gasped, breathless from the flight and fear.

For a moment, it looked like Jet was going to argue with her. He got that furrow between his eyebrows, the one that said he was thinking hard, and an argument seemed inevitable. But then he glanced over her shoulder, and he didn't seem to like what he was seeing. His eyes widened.

"Run!"

He grabbed her hand and pulled before the word was fully out of his mouth, and she didn't resist. They leapt into the scrubby bushes that lined the road, crouching down as far as they could as they ran. Maybe it was her imagination, but Sally could swear she heard the hum of electricity coming from the car, and she wanted badly to turn around and see what it was. At least she knew Frankie Ratchet wasn't firing the Neural Stimulator at them. You had to stab someone with it, and they were out of range. They were safe from that, at least.

Unless that thing also had a trigger...

She didn't like that thought at all. As they entered the tree line, she pushed herself harder despite the fire in her lungs. Jet led the way, and branches whipped back at her as she followed him. Her cheeks stung from getting repeatedly whacked in the face. She threw up her arms in an attempt to protect them, but no soap.

"Hide?" asked Jet. His face was flushed; his sides heaved. Under different circumstances, she might have teased him about it, but she didn't have enough breath for a full sentence either.

"My house."

He arched a brow but didn't argue, which was good. With every moment that passed, Sally got more and more worried about Ma and the baby. How had Frankie Ratchet known where to find her? Maybe James told him where she went to school, but maybe not. If he'd gone to their house, and found Ma? She couldn't bear to think about it.

They had to lose him and get home to warn Ma. She couldn't hear any sounds of pursuit, but that didn't mean it wasn't happening. Maybe Frankie Ratchet had a sound dampener. Maybe he had *rocket boots*.

That thought was enough to give Sally's feet wings. Too bad that was just a saying and wasn't really true.

A few minutes later, huffing and puffing with exertion, they sprinted into the house, the door swinging shut behind them with an ear-splitting bang. Sally winced, waiting for Ralphie's hiccupping cry, which would probably be followed by hollow coughs and Ma's angry yells. It was not a good way to start off this conversation, but Sally had to make her listen. Ma *had* to believe her, because things were getting dangerous.

But there was no crying, coughing, or yelling. The house was still and silent. She knew her brothers were off doing their chores, because that's what they did after school every day. But Ma and Ralphie should have been home. The fact that they weren't made Sally's heart beat even faster than it already was after their pell-mell flight from Frankie Ratchet's car. She scrambled toward the kitchen, tripping over the sofa en route and nearly ramming her head into the door. Jet hauled her up with a worried look on his sweaty face.

"What is it?" he hissed, watching the door like a whole herd of bad guys with strange devices might pop through it at any moment.

"Ma..." Sally squeaked out, but then she had to shut her mouth because she felt like crying and she didn't want to be such a *girl*. Besides, if Ma and Ralphie were in trouble, blubbering wasn't going to help.

She finally burst into the kitchen. The swinging door screeched loudly and finally settled into silence. She made a distracted mental note to oil the hinges if she didn't die first.

The kitchen was still and silent. Between the darkened lamps and the closed curtains, it felt dark and funereal. Not even the presence of a cooling pie on the counter could make her feel better, and Ma's pie was one of her favorite things ever. For her eleventh birthday, Ma had made her a cherry one all for herself. She'd eaten it right out of the pan and taunted her brothers with every bite.

Wait. There was a note on the counter. Sally grabbed it and scanned it quickly, squinting in the dim light but not willing to wait the extra two seconds it would take to open the curtains. Luckily, Jet was there to back her up. He threw them open and completely blinded her in the process. But finally, she could make the words out.

"Gone to get more kerosene for Ralphie. Back by dinnertime. – Ma"

All the breath went out of her in a relieved whoosh, and she sat down at the kitchen table without quite meaning to. It was like her legs suddenly decided they couldn't take the pressure, and they weren't going to stand for this kind of treatment anymore.

"Are you okay? Is there something wrong with your Ma?" Jet hovered worriedly at her elbow.

She shook her head. "They went to get Ralphie's medicine. That's all."

"Oh." He eyed the pie on the counter. "Do you think she'd mind if we cut that?"

Sally snorted. "Yeah, she'd mind. Get an apple from the bin. We need to have a talk with James. If his metal robot thing is going to keep attracting gangsters, he's got to get rid of it."

"Metal *whatsit*?"

They sat at the kitchen table, munching on apples and peanut butter, while she explained what had happened the night before. Jet took it surprisingly well. Maybe because it was hard to deny the existence of metal men after seeing your lifelong enemy hit by a weapon that made him think he was a duck.

"So that's why that Frankie Ratchet chap showed up today," said Sally. "I was hoping they'd leave us alone after last night, but I think they still want their robot thing back."

"Yeah, but it's broken."

"We know that. But they don't." Sally pulled a face at him. "And besides, it's not theirs."

"So you're gonna fight them for it? I don't know, Sally…"

"If I have to choose between the robot and keeping my family safe, of course I'll choose my family. I won't like it, but I'll do it." She sighed. "I just want them out of our faces."

Jet probed at the blackened skin under his eye and winced. "Agreed. 100%. Mine's pre-damaged; it doesn't need to get worse."

It only took a few moments for them to make their way to the back of the house and shove open the door to James's old bedroom, but by that time Sally had worked herself into a nice snit. This whole thing was his fault. If he hadn't taken the metal man, none of this would have happened. If he had just told someone about it instead of trying to bury it in the yard, none of this would have happened. The whole thing stunk, and on top of everything else, she'd lost the chance to take apart a Neural Stimulator and see how it worked. Frankly, she was more than a little tempted to neurally stimulate *James* and see how he liked it.

But his room was empty. Sally was much more than a little tempted to punch something, or maybe take all the sheets off his bed and stomp on them for a while, but that wasn't very mature. She contented herself with sticking her tongue out at the entire room to convey her complete dissatisfaction with anything James-related. She was just about to go hunt him down when she saw the sheet of paper on the pillow. Because apparently James couldn't just add his message to Ma's note. Oh, no. He had to have his own.

She rolled her eyes and picked it up only to find that this was definitely not her brother's usual chicken scratch. The letters were black and blocky, and in places the writer had stabbed the paper so hard that the pen went straight through.

It said: "We have your brother. Bring the robot to the Golden Pagoda in Chicago. Tonight. 8 PM. Or else."

Jet stood on tiptoe to read the note over her shoulder and snorted. "That's a crock of..." but then he realized that she wasn't laughing along with him. "It's not real, is it, Sally? I mean, James is just playing a joke on you."

"If it was Henry, I'd believe it. But James? He doesn't think that way."

She sat down heavily on the bed, and after a short moment of hesitation, Jet settled down next to her and put an arm around her shoulder.

"Are you sure?" he asked. "I mean, maybe Henry's the one playing the joke, right?"

"This isn't his handwriting," she said miserably. "Those Steel Syndicate men took him, Jet. I just know it. They took him while we were off talking with Frankie Ratchet. I knew he didn't want to offer me a real job. It was just a distraction." She couldn't keep the bitterness out of her voice.

"I don't know about that, Sally. He sounded awful serious to me. Besides, if he didn't want to offer you a job, why didn't he just tell you they had James and you had to bring the robot? They didn't have to go through all that rigmarole."

"Maybe." She shrugged. "It doesn't matter anyway. I'm not working for a bunch of yahoos who kidnapped my brother."

"What are you going to do?" he asked. "And how can I help?"

"What else can I do?" She sniffled but refused to let the tears fall. She was just so scared. "I have to take them the robot and save my brother. I could wait for Ma to get back from town and tell her everything, but if I do, I'll probably miss the last train. You know she likes to shop around Patterson's Goods and Sundries until they kick her out. If I don't show up, who knows what will happen to James?"

"All right." Jet thought for a second. "Should I go get your brothers?"

"No. They'll just try to stop me. I'll deliver the robot and bring James home tonight, and no one will be the wiser. That's how I want it, okay?"

"I guess," Jet said reluctantly. "But what's the plan? You don't really think these goons are going to let you waltz in, drop off the robot, and just leave, do you?"

"No. And it's too heavy to carry by ourselves."

They sat there glumly for a few minutes, each of them hoping that the other would come up with a brilliant idea to save the day. With every passing moment, Sally got more and more discouraged.

Suddenly, she thought of something. It was reckless. It would never work. She'd be nuts to try it, but there wasn't anything else.

So she took a deep breath and said, "I think I have a plan."

"Of course you do, Calamity," Jet said gleefully. "Just tell me what to do."

So she did.

CHAPTER 11

Sally and Jet left for the train station before anyone returned to the Slick household, which Sally felt was for the best. She'd left yet another note on the kitchen counter claiming to be eating dinner at Jet's house. It was an alibi that would probably hold—if only they could get out without anyone seeing her white, stressed-out expression or the robot they were pushing on a cart she'd devised by outfitting an old table with wheels. While Jet went for the train tickets, she'd spent a few minutes tinkering in her workshop, making the necessary modifications that would hopefully get them out alive. The finished product was a lot lighter than the original, for one thing. That was very helpful; as it was, the two of them struggled to get it up onto the jury-rigged cart.

The train ride was fairly uneventful, except for the skeptical looks from the other passengers who, for some reason, didn't believe that two kids would be transporting a wheeled table full of scrap metal to the city. As a cover story, it did lack something. They got strange looks even before one of the metal man's arms fell off the cart at one point and latched onto some old lady's leg. She got off the train at the next stop, and the other passengers gave them a wide berth after that. They had an entire half of the train car all to themselves. It was pretty nice.

When they got off at the Chicago train yard, Sally nearly got trampled by the other passengers right outside the doors. She barely noticed as Jet pulled her and the robot's cart to safety. She'd never been to the city before. It was so *big*. And loud. And there were machines everywhere, clanking and hissing and throwing off clouds of smoke into the air. She saw trucks and cranes, transporting heavy boxes onto empty train cars. Off to one side, a workman in thick safety glasses worked on a wall with some kind of motorized tool that she itched to get her hands on. As they crossed the platform, her eyes danced from machine to machine, and she modified each one in her mind, adding filters and redesigning venting systems to better aeration and, in one case, mentally adding a coat of pink paint. Hey, that's what the thing called for. It wasn't her fault.

The people were somewhat secondary to her, as evidenced by the fact that she wasn't watching where she was going and kept barging into them. She earned more than a few angry mutters, and one wild-haired man with black-stained fingertips stopped clean in his tracks when she ran over his foot with the cart. He seemed about to yell at her, and then his brows drew down as he studied their little procession. He turned around and stalked off, pulling his white jacket around him. She almost yelled after him to ask what kind of idiot wears a white coat to a train yard full of soot but decided against it.

"Weird." Jet jerked his chin toward the man in the white coat. Sally wasn't sure if he meant the man's behavior or his clothing, but she nodded anyway. "So where are we going exactly?" he continued.

She pulled out the Chicago street map that James had sent for Christmas. At the time, she'd thought it was a terrible gift, especially since he'd gotten her and each of her brothers the exact same thing, whereas she'd spent months painstakingly crocheting each of her siblings a lumpy but personalized stocking cap. But now she was beginning to appreciate the usefulness of the map. It was certainly better than the previous year when he'd gotten her a set of lace doilies. What in the heck was she supposed to do with those?

It was all but impossible to push the cart and read the map at the same time, especially in these crowded streets. She was pretty sure that, just on this street, she could see more people than lived in Nebraska Township, and that thought was more than a little intimidating. How were they supposed to find James in this huge metropolis? They couldn't even figure out how to get to the Golden Pagoda despite studying the map during the entire train ride. The city was just so huge. Even if they did manage to figure out where they were going and make the exchange, then they'd have to make their way back to the train yard in the dark, and the whole thing was a recipe for disaster even if you didn't count the possibility that they might miss the last train and school the next day. She'd get a whupping for sure.

It seemed pretty selfish to be worrying about herself since she wasn't the one who'd gotten kidnapped, but she couldn't stop. Every time she forced herself to quit thinking about *that*, another worry crowded in, and she found herself staring at the tightly crowded lines of the map and chewing on her lower lip like somehow making herself bleed might fix the mess they were in.

"So what do we do next?" asked Jet, and he didn't sound worried at all. In fact, his face was bright with excitement.

"Aren't you..." Her voice came out weak and cracking, so she cleared her throat and tried again. "Aren't you nervous at all?"

"Of course not."

"Hmph. You're probably playing Jet Blackwood and Calamity Sue again. This is *real*, Jet. Really real."

"Of course it is, dummy." He punched her lightly on the arm. "I'd rather adventure with Sally than with Calamity any day. You're the brains behind the whole operation anyway."

"Thanks," she said, feeling absurdly flattered.

"So where to?"

The complete confidence in his voice shook her out of her fit of nerves. She glared down at the map like she was going to make it cooperate whether it wanted to or not. Sadly, the glare didn't work. It still refused to cough up the instructions to get to the Golden Pagoda. She turned it this way and that, trying to make sense of it, and then she realized—this city was just one big machine run by people like rats on a wheel. And the map in her hands? It was a schematic.

Suddenly, it felt like all the noise and all the hustle were purposeful. There was a music to the city just like any other engine, and it all fit together like the pieces of a jigsaw if you only listened. And if Sally knew anything, it was machinery. She looked down at the map again, puzzling out how all the pieces fit together, the neighborhoods flowing one into another and the street names hinting at their contents. Certainly the residents of Old Crabbe Bottom Street wouldn't ever be welcome at the estates on Kensington Court. Her eyes darted from one location to another, and finally settled on Chinatown.

"Here." She stabbed the map with her finger. "The Golden Pagoda has to be somewhere in this neighborhood. All we have to do is get there and find someone to ask for directions. How hard can it be? And it seems like there should be a trolley. James talked about them in his letters. I'd put it over here." She jabbed the map again and then dashed off through the crowd, completely forgetting about the cart until Jet shouted.

"Hey!" he yelled. "Forgetting something?"

"Whoops." That would have been bad, to lose their only bargaining chip. Not to mention their only weapon.

She blushed a little, and then he blushed, and for some reason that made her blush all the more. It all seemed so stupid, because this was Jet for god's sake, and Jet wasn't a blush-worthy kind of boy even if she was that kind of girl—which she wasn't. But here she was, doing it anyway, and she couldn't seem to stop.

Luckily, he broke the moment before she could die of embarrassment. "You want to lead the way?" he mumbled, shuffling his feet. "I can follow with the cart."

She nodded gratefully. "Sure. I'll go slow so you can keep up without running over any old ladies."

They both chuckled, but it was that forced kind of laughter you shove out when you're really feeling uncomfortable, and that stunk. Sally had never felt uncomfortable with Jet, and she didn't like it at all. The only thing to do was to forge on and pretend that the little bit of awkwardness hadn't happened in the first place. This was made much easier by the fact that the trolley stop wasn't in the most obvious place where it would reduce foot traffic and provide ideal access to the rest of the system—city, actually. It was a good fifteen feet off course, and she felt much better after she'd had a chance to loudly complain about what nincompoops the engineers were.

They got on to the poorly designed trolley system without much trouble after that—some nice man with a giant beard helped them lift the cart onto the trolley—and in a short amount of time, they found themselves at the entrance to Chinatown. It was exotic and bright and quite frankly scary as heck. Sally knew that the characters in the adventure magazines weren't all that realistic. No way could a hero be drowned, dragged behind a herd of rampaging bulls on the streets of Pamplona, and then dangled off the wings of an aeroplane while fist fighting with a whole gang of villainous thugs. He'd die of exhaustion first. And she knew that this logically meant that Chinatown wasn't as full of villainous thugs as the stories suggested. But that didn't mean that she wasn't scared stiff at the thought of going in, because there was at least one thug there, and he had her brother. But there was nothing to be done about that other than getting it all over with as quickly as possible.

Stepping onto the street felt like entering another world. The buildings all had weird shapes. The edges of the roofs curled up to the sky, glistening with lacquer. Incomprehensible signs stood at street corners and above mysterious shops with unknown dried *things* hanging in the windows. Buildings were dotted with stone dragons. As Sally and Jet crept their tentative way down the street, she saw one with glittering jeweled eyes that looked for all the world like it was watching her.

If that didn't make her nervous enough, the people did. They looked at her and Jet, and they jabbered quickly back and forth to each other in what she assumed was Chinese. She knew they were probably just wondering what on earth a pair of white kids were doing there, but a part of her—a small and paranoid part—was certain they were trying to decide how much to charge for them on the black market.

Finally, one member of the brightly colored throng approached them. He was wearing slippers and an intricately patterned silk robe, right there on the street. She'd never seen clothes so fancy. Embroidered over his heart was a pretty flower with dark green, curled petals. Half his teeth were missing, and his head was shaved with the exception of one long strand. Sally had a sudden, intense urge to pull on it. She resisted. Barely.

He bowed low before them. "Where do you go, young Master and Miss? Lost?" he asked, his words accented but understandable.

Sally let out a breath, and all the tension went out with it. For some reason, finding one person they could communicate with made all the difference. Suddenly, the darkening streets didn't look so ominous.

In fact, as the sun began to fall, she saw people lighting multicolored lanterns strung up from practically every available surface. This wasn't a place to fear. It was like being in an exotic fairyland where adventure might lurk around every corner.

"Excuse me, sir," she said, using her best manners. "We are trying to find the Golden Pagoda. Can you help us?"

She expected him to nod and smile and beckon them down the street, but he frowned instead. "Golden Pagoda no place for children. Especially not at night," he replied.

"But..." she searched for an explanation. She was fairly certain that he wouldn't believe her if she said she had to deliver a metal man to the gang of thugs holding her brother hostage. Frankly, when she put it that way, she had a hard time believing it herself.

"We have a delivery," Jet interjected. His chest puffed out proudly and he held himself with the kind of assurance she associated with long summer days of pretend adventures. It was the kind of attitude that usually resulted in his face getting pounded after school, but for once, it seemed to actually work. The man in the robe squinted at him, cocking his head curiously.

"What is...delivery?" The man stumbled over the unfamiliar word.

"Delivery. We have to take this to the Golden Pagoda." Jet gestured to the cart with its blanket swaddled cargo. "It has to be there by 8 PM."

"Please, sir. Will you help us?" asked Sally. "It's awfully important. A matter of life and death."

He considered her again and finally sighed in resignation. "Yes, Lingyu Gao will help."

"Thanks awfully, Mr. Gao!" Jet grabbed the man's hand and pumped it furiously. Lingyu Gao looked so shocked that even Jet noticed; he stopped immediately. "Um...sorry?"

After a moment, Lingyu Gao gave him a gap-toothed smile. "Is okay. In Chinatown, we bow. Like so." He demonstrated a deep bow right there on the sidewalk, and no one looked at him twice. Both Sally and Jet mimicked him as best they could. "I am Master Lingyu. You are?"

"I'm Sally Slick, and this is Jet Black."

"I will take you to Golden Pagoda, Miss Slick. Master Black. This way."

Master Lingyu wasn't particularly young, but he couldn't have been too old from the way he hopped nimbly off the sidewalk and led them across the street. Sally tried to memorize the way back, because it wouldn't do any good to save James if they couldn't find their way back to the train station again, but they took so many twists and turns through cramped alleyways, and there were so many strange and wonderful things to look at that she soon lost track of the way. Hopefully Master Lingyu or some other helpful English-speaker would be willing to point them back in the right direction, or maybe James would know. One way or another, she reassured herself, they'd make it.

She almost believed herself, but there was still a roiling pit of nerves where her stomach ought to have been.

As they moved deeper into Chinatown, it got darker and darker. The sun sank down behind the exotic, strangely decorated buildings, leaving behind it a sky streaked with a few last traces of orange light. And the street they were on wasn't as bright and colorful as the others. She couldn't see a single paper lantern or golden painted storefront. Here, it was all darkened buildings and shadowed figures broken by the flickering light of candles in windows and the occasional dull glow of an oil lamp. It was the kind of place Sally imagined must be full of opium dens and kidnappers. Without quite meaning to, both of them crowded a little closer to Master Lingyu, although what one little man in a robe and slippers was supposed to do against a gang of crazed opium addicts, Sally didn't know.

"Is here," Master Lingyu finally said, gesturing. "Golden Pagoda."

They had come to the end of an alley. The dingy wooden building in front of them had a sign that swung lazily in the breeze, creaking in protest. She couldn't read it, obviously, but there was no mistaking the grimy painting of a pagoda on it. It might even have been golden at one point. There were no windows to speak of, but through the thin walls, Sally could hear the noise and bustle of rowdy men inside. Her nervousness must have shown on her face, because Master Lingyu frowned at her again. "We can leave."

"No." She shook her head. James needed her, and she couldn't just abandon him. But she did make a mental note to kick him at the first possible opportunity.

"I will wait." Master Lingyu crossed his arms and stood next to the door, looking about as immobile as one of those stone gargoyles she'd seen all over the place. If she hadn't been so nervous, she would have kissed the old man. But as things stood, she just nodded gratefully.

"Thank you," she said, and she swallowed with difficulty over the nervous lump in her throat. "Jet? Bring the cart."

"Got it!" he said brightly, like they weren't about to enter a room full of potentially dangerous thugs that might decide to shoot at them, or neurally stimulate them, or any other number of unpleasant things.

With that in mind, Sally opened the door.

CHAPTER 12

The inside of the Golden Pagoda was pretty much what Sally had imagined. Dingy, loud, and full of drunken men staring blearily at empty glasses. It was the kind of dim that allowed bad guys to sneak up on you easily. The room was packed with people, difficult to see because of the haze of sickly sweet smoke that hung in the air. And it was loud—the kind of loud that makes you want to stick your fingers in your ears except that you know it won't make any difference. Jet tried anyway, but within moments he gave up the fight.

The moment Sally and Jet stepped through the door, all motion in the room stopped. They found themselves at the center of a circle of disapproving stares. Sally felt like she was being visually measured for her own coffin. Jet gave a little wave. Unsurprisingly, no one returned it. After a moment, the men went back to drinking and arguing and playing cards, but she still felt as if she was being watched.

Sally wrinkled her nose against the scent of unwashed bodies. Between that and the smoke and the noise, she was already getting a headache. She wanted to deliver the robot and get out before her brain decided to stage a revolt, but she had no idea where she was supposed to deliver it. She couldn't exactly walk up to every one of these ruffians and ask them if they were waiting for a robot delivery. So she stood on her tiptoes and tried to catch sight of someone she recognized. James or Frankie Ratchet, maybe. Sadly, the scar-faced mobster's presence would have reassured her. She'd seen him twice now, and he hadn't tried to kill her either time.

A greasy looking man with a greasy looking mustache and an even greasier shirt leaned down, stuck his face right into hers, and said something she couldn't understand. But by the way he was leering at her, she didn't want to know.

"Excuse me," she said, glaring at him.

But instead of giving way, he grabbed her. Jet yelled, "Hey!" behind her, but he had one hand on the cart and wasn't going to be much help. If he let go, someone might steal it. So Sally grabbed onto that mustache and yanked as hard as she could. A few strands came off in her hands, but not much, because it was as slick as it looked and her hand slid right off. Still, it seemed to hurt. The man released her and clapped his hand to his upper lip, screaming in wordless pain.

Unfortunately, that attracted attention. As in, the entire room fell silent, and every single head turned toward the pair of white-faced kids at the door. And this time, every expression was flat out angry.

"Uh...Sally?" Jet asked, clearing his throat nervously.

"We're looking for Frankie Ratchet," she said loudly, trying to sound like she wasn't quaking in her boots. Which she was, because she wasn't stupid.

The man with the patchy mustache went pale at the name, and he backed away from her, muttering what she thought might have been apologies. He bowed repeatedly and gestured, urging them to follow him. An aisle opened up before them, leading into the depths of the room. Sally wanted to run, but she knew there was no way she'd reach the door before one of them caught her. Besides, James was still count-ing on her. She had to keep reminding herself of what was at stake.

"Come on, Jet," she said.

Now that no one was trying to attack them, his nervousness disap-peared like it had never been there at all. He tipped an imaginary hat at her. "Rightio," he said, and then he pushed the cart along behind her. They ventured into the throng together, following the man with the patchy mustache.

Everywhere she looked, Sally saw dark, scarred faces with angry expressions, but none of them were Frankie Ratchet, and she was beginning to think maybe they'd gotten themselves trapped. Maybe he wasn't even here, and this was a trick designed to get rid of them and the evidence all at once? Or maybe the men who kidnapped James didn't work for the Steel Syndicate. Maybe they were from a rival gang, one whose leader wasn't like Frankie Ratchet at all. With every step, she got increasingly more nervous, but where could she go? Even the bartender behind his row of bottles looked like he belonged behind bars. And not the kind that served drinks.

But then, at the far end of the room, she saw a grimy table sitting in the middle of a wide, empty space, like all the Golden Pagoda goons were too afraid to venture close. Sitting at one end of the table was James, flanked by Frankie Ratchet, but she barely spared them a glance. Because sitting at the other end was a man with a metal face.

But it wasn't a robot like the one on the cart. That one had been all metal, and although she hadn't seen it in action, she had a good idea of how it would have moved—a little jerky, a little awkward. There were quite a few design improvements that she would have loved to make. But this man was quite obviously flesh and blood. His neck and hair looked just like a normal person—a thin, almost scrawny neck and a perfectly coiffed shock of black hair—but the oval of his face was covered by a shiny metal mask, punctuated by a pair of eye holes, nose holes, and a slitted mouth. It fit tight to his skin, so tight that it looked fused on.

But the most extraordinary part came when he greeted her. "Sally Slick," he said, and the mouth *moved*.

It wasn't like the hinges of the robot on the cart. This was the suppleness of skin turned metal. His face moved and changed like flesh even though it was by all appearances made out of shiny steel. It was the most extraordinary thing she'd ever seen. She wanted to rip it off his face, mostly because she wanted to know how it worked but also because it was completely unfair that a bad guy would have something so cool.

"We brought your metal man," she said. "Give me back my brother." Jet elbowed her in the ribs, hard, hissing a warning under his breath. "Please," she added reluctantly.

The man with the steel face scowled at her, and she made a mental note to be a little more polite. There was still a chance that they might negotiate something, right? And if not, well, she was prepared for that. He gestured to the seat opposite him.

"Sit down, Miss Slick," he said.

She glanced at James, wanting nothing more than to drop off the robot, grab her brother, and make for the door. But it didn't take a genius to realize that wasn't going to happen. Her brother's wrists were shackled together, and a chain ran from the cuffs under the table. Between that and Frankie Ratchet's restraining hand on his shoulder, he wasn't going anywhere until they said so. It was enough to make a girl angry, to see her brother like that, and it felt much better than being scared, so she went for it.

She frowned at the masked man but didn't feel like she had much choice when it came to sitting at the table with him. The rest of the thugs in the Golden Pagoda were no longer staring at them. In fact, they were looking anywhere but at that table in the back corner, and somehow that was more worrisome than being the center of attention. If these rough fellows didn't want to see what might happen, it must be very bad indeed. Well, she'd give them what for. She had a surprise up her sleeve that none of them expected. No one messed with Sally Slick's family and got away with it.

So she sat.

"I am the Steel Don." He offered a hand for her to shake. Sally would have bet that the golden signet ring on his finger could have paid for all of Nebraska Township and maybe a couple of the surrounding towns too.

She folded her hands on the table and stared at his outstretched arm. "You have my brother in chains," she said.

The Steel Don glared at her. "Why won't you shake my hand?"

"You have my brother in chains," she repeated, stressing each word.

"He kept trying to escape," interjected Frankie Ratchet. "It's nothing personal."

"Not at all." The Steel Don sneered. "We thought you would be happier with the chains. The other option was to beat him unconscious and throw him in the lake."

Sally knew this was just an attempt to intimidate her, but the stricken expression on James's face hit her hard. For a moment, fear and anger struggled for control. In the end, fear won. It would have gone very badly if Jet hadn't intervened.

"That is a load of rubbish," he proclaimed. "Your goons shot up her home. Then you kidnapped her brother, and then we had to cart this two ton lug of bolts all the way here on the train, and instead of saying 'thank you' like a decent person, you start off by threatening us?"

Frankie Ratchet blinked. James coughed so hard he nearly choked on his own tongue. His chains clanked as he tried to bring his hand to his mouth, but there wasn't enough give.

"Take the chains off, or this conversation is over," Sally said, her nerves bolstered by Jet's display of bravado.

The metal mouth frowned at her. "You are giving me an order? Don't you know who I am?"

"You're the Steel Don, and you're holding my brother hostage. What else do I need to know?"

"I do not like your attitude, young lady." The Steel Don's fingers clenched, and he actually growled at them. He had even less of a sense of humor than Miss Cranston, and that was saying something. Sally glanced at his ears to see if steam might come out. With most people, that was just a saying, but since the guy had a metal face she thought it was an actual possibility. Sadly, there was no steam to speak of.

Frankie Ratchet cleared his throat. "Miss Slick," he said, "perhaps you might reconsider your answer to my earlier question?" He changed the subject smoothly, and it seemed to work. The Steel Don fell into quivering silence, watching her.

"What question?" she asked cautiously.

"Would you work for us? The Don is very eager to have the brightest minds in his organization. You've seen what we're capable of. I know you're interested. Your eyes betray you."

"Yeah, well, so what if I am?"

"Sally wouldn't work with kidnappers," interjected Jet.

"We are not kidnappers. James is an employee of our organization," said the Steel Don. His voice was...well, steely.

"Do you normally pick up your employees at gunpoint and slap them in chains? Because that's just not ducky, mister. I think I'll pass on the offer of employment," said Sally. She knew she was picking a fight, and that wasn't smart, but how stupid did they think she was? "What kind of organization treats people like that?"

"We're the syndicate that will rule Chicago in the next few months, Sally," said Frankie Ratchet. He produced a ring of keys from his pocket as he talked and began to remove James's restraints. "You've seen what we're capable of. Come work with us. We'll get you better schooling than you'd ever get in Nebraska."

"Township."

He blinked. "Pardon?"

"I live in Nebraska Township. Illinois. If I lived in Nebraska, none of this would have happened." She sighed longingly.

"Whatever, kid. We'll give you the kind of workshop you can only dream of. Equipment galore! This is the kind of opportunity you can't afford to shrug off. A mind like yours doesn't belong on a farm. You know it doesn't."

Despite everything that had happened—the guns and the fear and the metal faced madman across the table—she couldn't help but consider it. She knew, just *knew*, that she was destined for something great. She felt it in her bones, and her worst middle-of-the-night fear was that she'd never get the chance to do it. How could she become a great inventor when all she had to work with were rusty scrap parts and scrounged up tools? And what chance did she have—a small town farm girl—to get the kind of education that would open doors for her? What good were amazing inventions if they never made it out of their tiny backwater town? The Steel Don was crazy for sure, but Frankie Ratchet didn't seem quite so bad when she thought about it. She could work directly for him, couldn't she?

But then, James started massaging his wrists with a wince, and she realized that since she'd entered the room, he hadn't even said a word.

"James?" she asked. "Are you okay?"

He took in a shaky breath and let it out. Then he nodded. But he still didn't speak, and that frightened her more than anything else had. He'd never missed a chance to lay down his opinions before, especially to his younger siblings. Either something was really wrong, or he was messing with her. And if that was the case, she was tempted to leave him in the Golden Pagoda with the crazy man.

"Do you still have your tongue?" She arched her eyebrow.

He let out a startled laugh. "Yeah," he said. His voice sounded shaky and almost near tears. "I didn't think you'd come."

"What kind of thing is *that* to say?" she demanded, and she probably would have launched into a complete tirade if it weren't for Jet's restraining hand on her arm. "Never mind."

The Steel Don shoved his chair back with a clatter and stood up from the table. "This conversation bores me. You will accept my offer of employment, or you will not leave this building alive. Take your pick. I leave now."

He walked away from the table toward the front door. Sally couldn't help it. She stuck her tongue out at his back. When she turned back, she saw that James had his head on the table. His shoulders shook with silent sobs. That more than anything made her realize that this was serious—this crazy man really would have them killed just because she'd refused him. She felt scared but resolved. She wanted to pat her brother on the shoulder and tell him that she wasn't stupid, that she'd planned for this kind of situation, but she couldn't afford to give up the element of surprise. All she could do was reach under the table and give Jet's knee a squeeze. He knew what to do.

Frankie Ratchet gave her a sympathetic smile. "I'm sorry, missy. I know you have no reason to believe me, but I truly am. I tried to avoid this kind of a situation, but you wouldn't listen to reason."

"Your boss is the one who needs to listen to reason, Mr. Ratchet. He's loopy. Why on earth would someone like you work for somebody like him?" she asked.

He shrugged. "He's the most prominent crime lord in the city. Ruthless and intelligent and determined. I can ride on his shadow to the top of the town, and if I can do a little good along the way, that's a mighty fine thing." He took his cigarette case out of his pocket and flipped it open. "I'd make sure to take you under my wing, you know. You'd never have to see the Don at all if you took the deal."

"And if I don't?"

"It won't be pretty, kitty. I wish it could be different, but there are some lines I can't cross."

"I understand." She hung her head, and she was just about ready to push the button, the one on the device she'd stashed in her pocket, when she heard a shout from somewhere near the door.

"Miss Slick! Master Black! You okay?"

It was Master Lingyu. He pushed his way through the crowd, and for some reason, the toughs fell away before him the same way they had before the Steel Don.

Frankie Ratchet rose to his feet as the old man approached. "You!" he shouted, his hand dipping into his pocket. "I should have killed you the last time."

"You could have tried," replied the old man with quiet dignity.

"Men, don't let him leave this place alive!" said Frankie Ratchet.

There was a calculated, assessing pause, like the calm before a storm, and then every man in the room fell on Master Lingyu. They leapt out of the shadows, swinging fists or bottles or dingy knives, teeth bared in savage fury. Some shouted taunts that Sally couldn't comprehend, although her mind filled in horrible translations. Master Lingyu became a blur of colored silk, twisting and weaving in a strange dance that left his attackers reeling in his wake. Sally and Jet took shelter behind the cart as men leapt over their heads to join the fray. One of the assailants was tossed like popcorn on an open flame and went flying back to where he came from, nearly clipping Sally in the face with his foot as he flew.

It seemed like the ideal time to make their escape. Everyone was distracted. No one would know they were gone. All she needed was to collect James and flee. Where was he? She inched her head up to look, and a bottle shattered on the cart, flinging stinging liquid into her eyes.

She rubbed it away with her sleeve and tried to ignore the burning sensation. At least it hadn't been glass. She tried again, peering about in the dim and the din as quickly as possible. She couldn't believe what she saw.

"James!" she hissed. Her brother was still sitting at the table, frozen with fear, his eyes wide and shocky. No matter how many times she called his name, he wouldn't move. He only flinched as a knife flew past his head.

"Stupid idiot." She leapt toward him and made it almost to his side before a man fell on top of her, crushing the breath from her body. At least the sight of his sister being pulverized by two hundred pounds of greasy goon shook James out of his stupor; he kicked the unconscious man off to the side, and they both joined Jet in his hiding place as the fight raged on.

Master Lingyu may have been a martial arts terror, but he was only one man—and an old one at that—and for every assailant he dispatched three more took his place. A bottle flew toward him just as one of the knife-men slashed at his belly. He avoided the blade but was just a fraction of a second too slow in deflecting the projectile. It clipped the side of his temple. Blood began to stream down the side of his shaved head, pattering on the floor.

"Jet," she said, pulling him close enough to hear. "On the count of three, push the cart into the corner. I'm pushing the button, and we're getting out of here."

He nodded, his expression flickering between pants-wetting excitement and pants-wetting fear.

"Button? What?" asked James, his arms curled up over his head.

"Just trust me," she said. "On my mark, follow Jet and make for the door."

The old James would have argued, but after all that had happened, he seemed to realize that he couldn't get away with it any more. He nodded, his lips setting into a familiar stubborn line. But at least he didn't argue.

"Tell me when you've got a clear shot for the corner, Jet," she said, her eyes on Master Lingyu. His movements were getting progressively slower and less dancelike. "We're better than these yahoos. We're not going to kill anybody just for the fun of it."

"Just a sec..." he said. "Wait...Wait...Now!"

He shoved the cart toward the corner. The long trip had done a number on one of the wheels. Frankly, she was surprised they'd held on as long as they had. They weren't built to support so much weight, and she hadn't had the time to reinforce them. The cart squealed in loud protest, wobbled, and then fell over, spilling the precious robot to the ground. It clattered and rolled further than one would expect given its weight. Sally hoped no one would notice.

"Go go go!" shouted Sally, shoving her brother with one hand. The other was in her pocket, fumbling with the rectangular transmitter she'd stashed there. She couldn't find the button, and one of the toughs was walking toward them with a knife. Maybe he was intending to stab her, and maybe he wasn't, but she didn't want to find out. Master Lingyu went down under a pile of goons. All was lost if she couldn't find the button.

The transmitter twisted in her fingers, almost like it had come to life. The button was suddenly, miraculously *there*. She pushed it.

The Golden Pagoda exploded.

CHAPTER 13

Sally knew their only hope of escaping the Golden Pagoda unharmed was to take the bad guys by surprise. They'd expected her to be a scared little girl. They hadn't expected her to throw together a dummy robot and put a tear gas bomb into its torso, and she was counting on the resulting confusion to help them make their escape. The dummy wasn't a perfect replica, but they hadn't even bothered looking under the blanket. They'd said they respected her talents, but they didn't really. Not yet. Not enough.

Sally had never expected to find herself making a bomb and hadn't had much idea how to begin. But after a lifetime of practical jokes, Henry was an expert on this kind of thing, and he was a Slick through and through. He'd kept detailed notes on all of his tricks. He'd used this particular bomb, made from chlorine tablets and rubbing alcohol, in the church cellar before services a couple months ago. The congregation lasted about two minutes before the fumes wafting up from the floorboards drove them outside with tears streaming down their faces.

None of the grownups could prove that Henry had done it, but he'd gotten whupped anyway.

Sally and Jet had one advantage in the seconds before she pressed the button and detonated the explosive—they knew it was coming and could prepare for it. Each of them took a long breath in the seconds before detonation, and they both donned a pair of work goggles to protect their eyes moments before she pressed the button.

The bomb hidden inside the robot's mangled torso went off with a loud bang, spraying shrapnel and a stinging greenish gas through the Golden Pagoda. It was louder than Sally had expected, or maybe that was just the result of setting it off in such a crowded space. It sounded like someone had set off a handful of firecrackers inside a tin can; there was a loud bang and the sound of tearing metal, and then bits of dull gray shrapnel began flying through the air. She hadn't anticipated that, and she didn't duck quite fast enough. A twisted bit of steel about the size of her fingernail struck her on the cheek just underneath the edge of the goggles. It felt like she'd been stung by a million wasps all at once. But as much as she wanted to roll around on the floor and cry, they had to get out, and they had to get out *now*. She clapped a hand to the wound and felt the slick wetness of blood trickling down her face.

In the aftermath of the detonation, the room was chaos. Tables were overturned, and broken bottles leaked foul smelling liquids into growing puddles. Men rolled on the floor, clutching various injuries, and she felt surprised more than anything else. She'd meant to stink them out. She hadn't intended to hurt anyone, and part of her felt vaguely guilty over the unintended damage, but they would have killed Master Lingyu if she hadn't done something. As things stood, she thought the shrapnel had been a lucky break on their part, even if it did nearly take her eye out.

Jet made a break for the door with James as they'd planned. She was supposed to follow them, but instead she made her way through the rubble to the inert figure of Master Lingyu. The old man was sprawled on the ground with his arms flung wide like he was ready to embrace the whole world. He had more bloody scratches and bruises than she could count, and there was no way to know how many of them were inflicted during the fight and how many he'd taken from her bomb. But there would be plenty of time to feel guilty later. She shook him wordlessly as the acrid smoke slowly began to dissipate, but all she got in response was a weak cough.

The only way to get him out was to carry him, and she had to hurry before someone recovered enough to try to stop her or before she fell over from lack of oxygen. She couldn't hold her breath any longer, and after one sip of air, her lungs immediately began to burn. She tucked her mouth into her shirt to filter the air a little and moved as quickly as possible.

She hefted his slight form onto her shoulders. He wasn't too heavy, but the slippery silk of his robes made it tough to get a good hold on him. As she struggled not to drop him on his head, a trio of goons staggered toward her, retching and gasping for breath in the slowly dissipating smog. They looked like they'd been beaten with sticks and rolled down a hill, but they still moved to intercept her, knives at the ready.

"Leave me," Master Lingyu said weakly, but there was no way she was going to do that, not after he'd risked his life to save them.

She kicked a chair toward their attackers, hoping to trip them up so she could reach the door, but it only took one of them down. The other two hopped the obstacle and grabbed her by the arms. Master Lingyu dropped to the floor with a wheeze and a grunt.

"Gotcha, girlie."

The man on her right leaned in close, his breath worse than the exhaust fumes of all the racing tractors put together. His face was streaked with tears, and he let out a hacking cough right in her face, spraying her with spit.

"The...Steel Don...will pay good...money for you," added the other, wheezing.

Sally strained against her captors, but she couldn't break free. In that moment, she forgot about the smoke, drawing in a breath to call to Jet for help. Big mistake. It was like filling her mouth with gasoline. She immediately began to choke, drawing more of the gas into her chest.

There was the sound of breaking glass, and suddenly her right arm was free. She lifted streaming eyes to see a man, probably as old as Master Lingyu if not older, break a bottle over the head of another thug. The dingy bar was overrun by old men in colorful silks, with long streaming mustaches and crazy martial arts moves. The one standing next to her had some familiar fancy embroidery on his chest: the green flower with the pretty curved petals. He must have been friends with Master Lingyu. Sally tried to smile at him but broke out into another round of coughing instead. The man who had saved her gestured in a come-hither way, but she shook her head, getting down on the floor next to Master Lingyu. She would carry him out if it killed her, and no amount of tugging from the other man would sway her from her task. She picked him up, finally, then coughed so hard that she threw up a little, and finally managed to stagger out into the cool evening air.

About five feet from the door, she began to choke again and nearly dropped poor Master Lingyu, who was probably beginning to wish that someone a little less dropsy had come to his rescue. Before it could happen, he was lifted from her back by a set of strong hands, and then someone started pounding on her spine the way people do when someone is coughing uncontrollably. She turned to see Jet thumping her on the back, as James helped settle Master Lingyu gently on the ground.

Both boys looked pretty winded, not to mention teary and sooty, but she'd never been so happy to see them in her life.

"Maybe next time you have to blow something up, it could involve a little less gas and choking?" rasped Jet.

She snickered uncontrollably until she puked again.

CHAPTER 14

At some point, Sally must have blacked out from lack of oxygen, because one minute she was on her hands and knees in the street outside the Golden Pagoda, retching into the gutter, and then she found herself inside a silk lined carriage. She could hear the familiar sound of horseshoes on cobblestones. The carriage jounced and rattled, but it was still much more comfortable than the gutter had been. Even better yet, Jet sat across from her, and her head rested on James's shoulder. They'd actually made it out alive.

"Where are we?" she asked. Her mouth felt mushy. It didn't want to cooperate with her, so the question came out more like "Whuh uh wuh?" But Jet didn't seem to have any problem understanding her. Apparently he was fluent in mush.

"Master Lingyu's friends offered to give us a ride so we don't miss our train. Isn't that neat?" he exclaimed. "They seemed pretty happy about you blowing up the place. I think they would have carried you on their backs if I'd asked."

"This is much better, thanks," she said wearily. She felt a little less numb, but more and more exhausted with every minute. It had been a long day, to say the least. "You okay, James?"

"Yeah." For a moment, he was quiet. "Thanks for coming for me, Sal. I wasn't quite sure how I was going to get out of that one."

"I don't understand why they took you. They knew the robot was damaged; they were the ones that shot it up, the idiots."

"Yes, but by that time, they'd had a look at your tractor and some of those other projects you have in that workshop of yours. They became less interested in BEM-1 and more interested in recruiting you."

"So they stole my brother." She snorted. "That's the stupidest recruitment technique I ever did hear."

"No kidding." James sighed. "Too bad you had to blow it up."

"Actually, not so much." She elbowed him. "It was just an empty casing. I have the real bot hidden away at home."

He beamed at her. "Good egg!"

She smiled at him wanly. It felt like her brains were sloshing around in her head with every bounce of the carriage. Focusing was impossible. It was frustrating until she realized that she'd have plenty of time to talk things over on the train. Maybe after a snack and a cold Pepsi-Cola, she might feel a little more together. Her stomach rumbled at the thought. It seemed like an eternity since she'd gotten home from school to find her brother gone. Had she eaten anything since her cheese sandwich at lunch? She didn't think so.

The carriage jounced to a stop, and James threw open the latch and led the way out the door. He helped her down the steps, where she was greeted by another Chinese man in bright embroidered robes. But compared to all the other silk robed men, this one was a baby. His mustache was only starting to turn gray at the base, and the curling hair didn't quite reach his elbows yet. He smiled brightly as she approached.

"Miss Slick," he said, in barely accented English, "it is my pleasure to convey you to this station for trains. All of the Order of the Jade Lotus are in your debt."

"I don't understand," she said, weaving a little on her feet. She just felt exhausted, that's all. And maybe, if she had to be honest, she'd gone a little overboard with the bomb. She still had a slimy taste in the back of her mouth from breathing in that gas. If she'd been alone, she would have spit on the street, but in polite company she'd at least attempt to be ladylike.

"The Order of the Jade Lotus is a secret society. We are charged by our grandmaster to fight the criminal tongs of Chinatown and keep the citizens safe," said the young man. "It is tough work, but easier because the gangs constantly fight each other for dominance, and none are successful. They weaken each other. But this Steel Don, he tries to unite all of the tongs under his leadership, in Chinatown and all across Chicago. If he is successful, all of Chicago is in big big trouble. He will be unstoppable."

"Are you sure?" She frowned. "He seemed pretty nutso to me. Will the other criminals really follow someone like that?"

"I am afraid so, Miss Slick. The Steel Don is unstable, but he is also ruthless and intelligent. The tongs believe he has magic on his side. They will follow him, out of fear if not respect."

"Magic?" she snorted. "Everyone knows that's not real."

"Do we?" The man arched a bushy brow. "You have seen his face. You have seen their metal men. The act of creating such a thing is magic, is it not?"

"Not hardly," said Sally.

"It's science," added James.

The siblings looked at each other in a rare shared moment of understanding. Sally couldn't keep from beaming, but James looked away uncomfortably. He'd never been able to handle public displays of affection.

"Science is magic with labels," the man declared. "You will see. There are things happening here that even science cannot explain. But they exist nonetheless, and the Steel Syndicate will exploit them to gain power if they are not stopped."

The man's face wrinkled with worry, and Sally wanted to ask a million questions. Even though her role in this strange adventure was over now, she was still curious. But then she heard the whistle of the train and the tinny voices of the conductors as they called for the final passengers to board for departure.

"We need to go, Sally," said James. "Or we'll miss the train."

Then Jet added, "But thank you, sir. Thank you so much." He grinned and bobbed up and down in what was probably supposed to be a series of bows, but it made him look more like a windup toy owned by a very grimy child. His hair stuck up in about twenty-seven different directions and was streaked with dirt, and a fragment of scrap metal was tangled up in it. Sally brushed it off for him and was rewarded with a one-armed hug.

"Go," the man gestured for them to move. "With our thanks."

"But what about Master Lingyu?" Sally asked, putting up a token resistance as her brother tried to drag her off. "Is he okay?"

"Lingyu is fine. Broken arm and cheekbone. Our doctor will care for him. Now go before you miss the train!"

"Oh good." Sally let out a relieved breath and waved. "Good-bye, then! Thank you for helping us! Maybe we'll see you again someday!"

They jogged toward the platform, and the few passengers left standing there got quickly out of the way. Either they were worried they might get run over or they didn't want any part of a gang of fragrant, grimy kids. Sally took one whiff of her shirtsleeve and realized she would probably have to burn the clothes. There was no way she was going to get the gassy smell out of them. The stench was so bad that they ended up with half a train car to themselves once again. It was nice to have the space to stretch out. She would have been quite comfortable if not for the fact that her stomach wouldn't stop rumbling.

After a particularly loud snarl, Jet said, "Gosh, I almost forgot!" He pulled something cylindrical out of his pocket. It was wrapped in waxed paper, but that didn't stop the most appetizing smell from wafting out of it. "One of the gents in the robes gave us some food. I don't know what it is, but it sure was good. I saved you some."

He handed it over, and Sally didn't waste any time. She unwrapped a crispy bread-like thing and began to chow down without hesitation. It was full of crunchy vegetable type things and spicy things and heavenly tasting things. She'd devoured about half of it before she remembered her manners and offered it sheepishly to the boys sitting across from her.

James smirked. "We already had ours. Besides, I'd be afraid to touch it. I think you might bite my hand off."

"No kidding," added Jet, grinning.

Under normal circumstances, Sally would have retaliated with a sharp comment or three, but there was food in her hands, and it was warm, and the spicy scent of it distracted her from the fact that she smelled like the inside of a cow barn. Worse, even.

She'd just taken a giant bite when the man sat down next to her.

She hadn't even heard him approach. All of a sudden, the seat next to her was occupied by a man in a white lab coat. He had food stains down the front of both his shirtfront and the coat, and his bow tie was askew, and his hair so wild that it made Jet's look tame. But his eyes behind the thick glasses were keen. They didn't seem to miss anything.

"Sally Slick?" he asked, his words heavily accented.

"Mmuph." She tried to cover her mouth, but a piece of unidentifiable vegetable went flying anyway.

"James." The man nodded at her brother.

"Good to see you safe and sound, sir."

James sounded—and looked—relieved. Sally swallowed the lump of food and wiped her mouth with the back of her hand.

"Who's this? You know him?" she asked in cautious tones. It's not that she was a complete scaredy cat, but the last people he'd brought home had tried to shoot her. Caution seemed wise.

"I am Doktor Proktor," the man proclaimed. His accent was hard and sharp, turning all the curvy Cs into hard Ks that sprayed spit into the air. She had no idea where he was from, but she bet they all wore spit guards there.

"Nice to meet you?" she said, not quite sure.

He shoved his hand toward her like it was a weapon. She shook it. He didn't even bother to bend his fingers around hers.

"I am the boss of James. You have my BEM prototype, yes?"

"Yeah." Her shoulders slumped. After all that work tricking the Steel Don into thinking they'd delivered the robot, now this so-called Doktor was going to take it right out from underneath her before she'd even had a chance to take it apart. It was so unfair.

"Ah, good," he said. "It is my gift to you."

"Sure," she said dully. "We can deliver it back to you—wait, what?!"

"It is for you." He nodded twice, the movement brisk and precise. "Yes, that is good. It will be your...what do you call it? The thing for when you take the new job?" He looked at James, head cocked to the side.

"A bonus?" James supplied.

Sally sat bolt upright, waving her hands desperately. "No, no, no. I've already had one crazy job offer today, thanks. Don't you people understand that I'm fourteen? I'll graduate from school when I'm seventeen, and then I can take all the jobs you'd like to offer me. But not until then. Thanks but no thanks."

The Doktor waved a hand, completely dismissing her. "Of course you are wanting the job. I shall teach you the making of robots.

You should see my new designs! I have undertaken the making of BEM-2, but I am convinced there are still design improvements to be made. With your help, it will be beautiful, yes?"

"I don't think you understand," she said, enunciating carefully. Because maybe he honestly *didn't* understand. The guy was awfully hard for *her* to understand with that accent and all, so she figured the opposite might also be true. "I can't move to the city to work for you. My parents won't allow that. I'm going to get into a ton of trouble as it is, getting home this late. And even if I could, I wouldn't work for the Steel Don. He's a complete crazy man."

"Pish. Doktor Proktor does not work for the Steel Syndicate." He leaned back into the seat like he belonged there, adjusting his glasses. "Doktor Proktor might use the Steel Syndicate for supplies, yes, and he might feed them a few mechanical morsels, but the best inventions he keeps for himself. Are you understanding this?"

"So you're using them." She wrinkled her nose thoughtfully.

"Well, yes. But is for the good of all things. Look—I will show you. I have invention you will love. Let me find it."

He began to rummage in his lab coat pockets, checking the left one, then the right, and then the left one again like the mysterious device in question might have teleported there while he was distracted. Unsurprisingly, he came up empty and threw his hands in the air like Ma did whenever she was exasperated. But thinking about Ma brought up all kinds of worries, like how Sally was going to explain her absence all day. Dinner at Jet's was one thing, but dinner time had been over hours ago. Hopefully Ma's happiness over seeing James would keep her from asking too many questions.

Doktor Proktor had no luck with the lab coat, so he moved on to various other pockets in his pants and shirt. It seemed like his clothes were one big pocket—how much stuff did one crazy-looking scientist guy need? Sally lost interest in the search and dove back in to the remains of her food.

"Aha!" exclaimed the Doktor. "Here it is! You must see this."

Sally had just stuffed a huge bite into her mouth. She turned around, chewing, just in time to see him pointing something that looked like a ray gun at her. It was made of a dull metal, punctuated by curled wires that ran from the grip to the pointy end of the muzzle, and that very same pointy end was currently pointing at her. It was the second time she'd been at the wrong end of a weapon in the past few days, and she was jumpy already. It took her two tries to swallow. Then she shrieked and threw up her arms, knocking the ray gun into the air.

"Don't shoot me!" she yelled.

"My Visionator!" exclaimed the Doktor.

CHAPTER 15

Everyone in the train car leapt out of their seats with alarm when Sally shouted about guns, but she'd knocked the weapon out of Doktor Proktor's hand so fast that no one else saw it. The passengers' fear quickly dissolved into angry mutterings. The Doktor went down on hands and knees, peering down the aisle in an effort to find his precious invention. While he was distracted, Sally ran up the aisle, trying not to feel like a complete coward. But she was outgunned, quite literally, and part of being a hero was knowing when to fight and when to flee, right? Jet seemed to think he was bulletproof; he shielded her retreat with his body, holding out his arms like they might stop any stray projectiles.

"Stop!" yelled the Doktor, still looking around the train car for the Visionator. "You will stop and listen to me, Sally Slick, or you will pay!"

That was enough to ignite the other passengers once again. They leapt to their feet and shouted for the Doktor to "Leave those kids alone!" But none of them moved an inch. Did they really think that yelling at the bad guys was going to accomplish anything? Apparently they did.

Sally turned to look over her shoulder. It wouldn't do to run for it and have Jet or James get killed instead. "Come on, Jet!" she urged. "James!"

But James's reaction stopped her in her tracks. Instead of following his sister to safety, he turned his back on her, crouching down to peer under the seats.

"I see it, Doktor!" he exclaimed, pointing. "The Visionator is right near that window, up against the wall."

"Good work, James!" The Doktor stood, smoothing his lab coat, and walked toward the window in question.

"James!" Sally hissed. "What are you doing?"

"Doktor Proktor is my boss, Sally. You shouldn't have hit him like that," her brother said, shaking a finger at her.

She couldn't believe what she was hearing. Hadn't that man just pointed a weapon at her? What was she supposed to do, let him shoot her just because he'd given James a job? And wasn't that job the very thing that had gotten them into this whole mess in the first place? If it wasn't for Doktor Proktor's plan to milk the Steel Syndicate for money, none of this would have happened. They wouldn't have gotten shot at. She wouldn't have had to bomb any buildings. He wouldn't have gotten kidnapped.

The whole situation was so shocking that she found herself completely flabbergasted and unable to figure out what to say. So she did the one thing she could do. She turned her back on James just as he had on her.

"Come on, Jet," she said. "Let's scram before someone else decides it's a good idea to shoot at us and then offer us jobs. Or the other way around. Anything with shooting, really."

The gray haired lady in the seat next to them looked at her oddly, trying to figure out if she was kidding or not. Sally didn't understand how anyone couldn't take this seriously. One look at Doktor Proktor, and she'd known he wasn't right in the head. Didn't anyone else notice these things?

At least Jet was with her, and he understood even if no one else did. He gestured for her to continue down the aisle first, still endeavoring to put himself between her and any sign of danger. And at that moment, there were a lot of signs of danger. Like the one where Doktor Proktor stood up with the Visionator in his hand and wild triumph in his eyes.

"Here!" he said. "I will show you of what I am talking, and you will understand it."

Sally worried that this demonstration might involve shooting her, which would not be a good thing. She sprinted the last few feet, stumbling as the train rocked beneath her, and began to fumble at the door between the cars. Unfortunately, she hadn't been on trains very often, and for once, her natural ability with mechanical devices failed her. She couldn't open the door. If she hadn't been so frightened, she would have felt really foolish. As it stood, though, she was so scared that her knees were shaking, and she fell back on the only weapon she had left—her mouth.

"Do you have any idea what you're saying?" She whirled around to face the mad scientist and rolled her eyes, giving it extra drama. "I honestly don't think you understand the words that are coming out of your mouth, do you?"

He actually paused, half lowering the weapon as the rest of the train car looked on in frozen fascination. So much for the adults coming to the rescue. Were they really going to sit around watching while she got shot, like this was some theater production? If so, they deserved to be smacked. If she'd had the time, she might have tried it, but she was too busy trying not to get dead.

"Pardon?" he asked.

Sally took a deep breath and launched in. "Well, after about a million years diagramming sentences with Miss Cranston, I can tell you that your sentence construction was completely wrong. Your pronoun didn't agree with your antecedent, and how are you supposed to let people know about your fabulous inventions if you can't communicate effectively?"

She folded her arms and stared him down, trying to look like she knew what she was talking about, although she was actually just doing her best impression of Miss Cranston. And to think Ma had always scolded her for not paying attention in class.

"Isn't that why I am wanting to hire you?" asked Doktor Proktor. "I did say this, yes?"

"I'm not sure you communicated that effectively, Doktor, as I said just a minute ago. And I think that communication is very important when negotiating things that are of utmost importance as this situation certainly is. You see..."

Sally kept on babbling, barely pausing for breath between sentences. She had no idea what was coming out of her mouth. It made no sense at all, but it seemed to be working. Doktor Proktor—and everyone else in the car for that matter—was staring at her with confusion. And all the while, her hand was behind her back, fumbling wildly with the latch. If only she could stall them until she could open the door, she and Jet might actually get out of this without being Visionated, whatever that meant.

Then the door seemed to open by itself. She lost her balance and nearly fell right out of the train car. She felt a breathless rush of vertigo as the train lurched under her feet and her hands scrambled for something to hold on to. She knew there was a safety bar outside the door so you couldn't just fall off the train without really making an effort, but she'd always had a natural talent for trouble. It didn't seem like something she wanted to risk, especially considering how her luck had gone over the past few days.

A pair of strong arms tucked under her armpits and hauled her back up to her feet. Wind turned the open doorway into a battleground as she was buffeted to and fro. She blew a wisp of hair out of her face as she struggled for balance, finally managing to right herself. Jet's face was white as a sheet, and he put a hand on her shoulder.

"Golly, Sal," he said. "That was close."

She nodded, looking gratefully at the heavily mustachioed train conductor who had hauled her to safety. His uniform was perfectly pressed, his posture ramrod-straight. He was definitely the kind of guy you wanted around when you were about to accidentally take flight off a train...or talk down a crazy scientist with a ray gun.

The crazy scientist didn't seem to appreciate the fact that he was no longer the center of attention. He waved his weapon around over his head like it was a lasso and might capture people's attention like a runaway steer. The most ridiculous thing about this technique was that it actually worked.

"You there. No weapons on the train. Put that thing down," said the conductor, moving in front of Sally and Jet. It was like a little parade of protection—he was covering Jet, who was covering Sally, who was covering...the door. Out of the four of them, at least the door was safe.

"You are needing to move from the way, sir," exclaimed Doktor Proktor, gesturing with the ray gun. "I am trying to show the girl how the Visionator is working."

"Put down your gun, or I'll remove you from my train." The conductor cracked his knuckles like he was itching for a fight.

"You don't understand, sir," James interjected eagerly from his spot flanking the mad scientist. "Doktor Proktor isn't going to shoot Sally. Not conventionally, anyway. The Visionator doesn't fire traditional bullets."

"No one will shoot anyone with any kind of bullets on my train. Now get off before I throw you off," the conductor repeated.

"Wait, what?" James sounded confused. "Are we stopping?"

"Nope."

"But..." Sally's brother looked around with an irate expression. "That's not fair."

"Trying to shoot a little girl isn't fair," said a fat man in a bowler, much braver now that someone else was handling the problem.

The prune-faced woman beside him nodded. "Yer getting off lucky, if you ask me. I think it's a pity lynching's not legal."

The handful of passengers, more secure with the authority of the conductor on their side, began to grumble ominously. Sally didn't want to see her brother thrown from the train, but she wasn't about to stop it from happening if that's the way things went. She'd already stuck her neck out for him—she'd made a *bomb* for him—and he'd thrown her to the wolves. No way would she make that same mistake again.

But Jet was a good egg. Much nicer than she was, anyway. He held up his hands and made his voice gentle the way he did when he was trying to coax her cat out of the tree again. Gadget liked high spaces even though he was such a meatball that he couldn't get down on his own.

"Here, now," Jet said, stepping forward. "There's no need to be hasty here. I'm sure that James and the Doktor can see reason." His voice had an instant calming effect on the group, and the lady with the prune face had the grace to look more than a little ashamed of herself. The conductor and Jet both relaxed as the tension dissolved. Sally was just happy that the two of them quit trying to smother her against the door. They didn't seem to think she needed shielding any more. Then Jet added, "All they have to do is give up the gun." His voice cracked on the last word.

The fat man let out a bark of laughter that startled Doktor Proktor. The scientist's whole body tensed, pressing the trigger of the weapon by accident. It hummed loudly, discharging a flare of violet light that struck Sally and quickly enveloped her entire body. It tickled terribly. Even her teeth tickled, and she fell to the dusty floor of the train, squirming and shrieking.

The rest of the passengers didn't understand what was happening. They saw a girl who had gotten shot by some weird ray gun, and she was screaming, and screaming generally meant that something bad was happening. They finally decided to do something about the man with the gun, even if that something came too late to save Sally.

"Get him!" yelled the fat man.

"He shot that girl!" exclaimed the prune-faced lady. "Throw him off the train before he can get the rest of us!"

The mob overtook the white coated Doktor, shoving James off to the side. Two of the passengers grabbed the Doktor by his arms, and the conductor snatched the weapon away and broke it over his knee.

The mad scientist howled with anger. "You will pay for that! How dare you destroy my invention?!"

But the passengers were in a frenzy now and beyond listening to his threats. They snatched Doktor Proktor by his shoulders and legs, raising him up into the air. Their captive struggled and kicked, spitting words in an unidentifiable, harsh language. But they wasted no time in opening the door at the far end of the train car. The wind whipped through the car once again, almost drowning out James's anguished howl.

"No! Don't kill him! I'll have nowhere to go!" he yelled.

He began to surge forward, fists clenched like he was going to try to fight them all despite the odds. Jet grabbed his coat sleeve as James passed by, and it slowed him down just enough to save him. The passengers threw the Doktor out into the scrub brush that ran alongside the track. James wailed again. Sally could hear him howling, dimly, but the tickly feeling had grown into a full body itch. It felt like little bugs were crawling all over her, and no amount of scratching would make them stop. The feeling was so intense that she found it impossible to concentrate on anything else.

As she lay there on the floor, scratching maniacally at her arms, James screamed wordlessly again, running to the still-open door at the far end of the train car. She knew he didn't deserve her help after everything he'd done, but she felt like she had to try. She stood up, still squirming in discomfort, and then realized that it actually helped to move around. The intense discomfort was starting to fade, and it seemed like the silly Visionator was just a trick. It probably didn't do anything at all. It was just a colored light in a fancy package. Frankly, she felt awfully silly for falling for it in the first place.

"James, the Visionator doesn't do anything," she said, rubbing the base of her spine against the door frame next to her, trying for one last impossible to reach itch. "He's just trying to trick you. This guy isn't worth your time. Come home with us, please?"

He turned to look at her, his face twisted so badly out of shape with hate that he looked like a total stranger.

"What do you know?" he spat. "You're just a stupid kid. You refused to work under the most brilliant inventor in the history of the universe. I may not be as good with mechanics as you are, but at least I'm not attempting to murder a certified genius. I think you're just jealous that he's better than you'll ever be."

"James, he got you into this whole mess," she pleaded. "I came all this way to save you, and then he pointed a *gun* at me. What was I supposed to do, let him shoot me? I didn't know it was fake."

"Fake? Hah! Wait until you see. Just you wait."

With that, he leapt off the train.

Sally rushed to the doorway he'd just vacated, tripping over a stray bag and nearly ending up in the lap of the portly man, who steadied her with a pitying expression on his face. "I'm sorry, lassie," he said, patting her on the shoulder, but there was no time for her to pause; the train still rumbled down the track and she had to know that her brother was okay before he was out of sight. Even after everything that had happened, he was still blood.

The door had closed automatically after James's mad leap, but this latch was much easier to open than the other one had been. She flung it open and leaned out to peer down the track, maintaining a death grip on the safety bar. The wind whistled past her, carrying a hint of stinging rain, and the night was full dark by now. She could barely see two shadows in the distance, walking away from the train. One limped, but otherwise they were alive and well.

Now that she knew he was okay, she could be angry with him. So she was.

CHAPTER 16

By the time Sally and Jet arrived back in Nebraska Township, it was almost 10 at night. They trudged home in the dark without words, because what was there to say? Sadly, the comfortable feeling didn't last long. As they walked up the lane toward the Black residence, Sally could see that all of the lights were lit, and Jet's dad's shadow paced to and fro behind the living room curtains. Her heart sank. All that trouble and worry for nothing. James was gone, and she was pretty sure that he wasn't ever coming back. She was also pretty sure that if he did, she was going to punch him in the mouth.

She felt angry and frustrated and exhausted, but none of that was Jet's fault. She didn't want him to get in trouble on her account, so she walked into the house with him and explained to Mr. Black that the late return home wasn't his son's fault. Jet stood there silently as she took all the blame, probably because she kept stomping on his foot every time he opened his mouth. Despite all her efforts to make herself the scapegoat in this situation, Mr. Black was still pretty angry until she told him how Jet had stood up for her against a whole herd of bullies (she may have exaggerated the story just a bit) and saved her from getting thrown off a train. His face filled with disbelief, so she repeated it all again. Then he was so pleased that he looked like he might burst. He stooped down to admire the battle scars on Jet's face and chucked him on the shoulder.

"I knew you had it in you, son," he said. "Don't you ever frighten me like this again, but I'm proud of you."

Jet couldn't stop blushing.

Sally smiled. "Yeah, he was pretty heroic, Mr. Black. I wish you could have seen it."

"Me, too." Mr. Black cuffed Jet's shoulder again. Sally couldn't quite understand how whacking someone on the shoulder meant congratulations, but she'd seen it from her brothers all the time, and Jet didn't seem to mind. "But now's the time for all young heroes to get their butts to bed, because they'll be going to school tomorrow morning, like it or not. Can I take you home, Sally?"

"No thank you, sir. It'll be just as quick if I cut through the back field, and I don't want to make trouble."

"Hoping to sneak in, are you?" At her shocked expression, Jet's dad grinned. He'd always been a cool cat, but this was unusual even for him. He really *was* impressed. "Don't you worry, missy. I won't spill the beans if you manage it."

Jet snorted. "Good luck. You're gonna need it."

She stuck her tongue out at him and resisted the urge to follow it up with a hug. Because while she might mean it as an I'm-glad-we-didn't-die-together-today hug, there was no guarantee that he'd pick up on that. And heaven forbid he might think it was a thank-you-for-coming-to-my-rescue-oh-knight-in-shining-armor hug. Under normal circumstances, she wouldn't have worried about it, but he was looking at her with those shining eyes, and she couldn't decide whether that was because he was seeing little hearts dance around her head or because he was two seconds away from falling unconscious on the floor.

So instead of hugging him, she shifted awkwardly from foot to foot a few times, cleared her throat, pretended Jet and his pa weren't looking at her like she was nuts, and waved goodbye.

"See ya tomorrow, Jet," she said. It felt pretty inadequate.

But all he said was: "See ya."

She let herself out the back door and cut across the yard, over the creek, and down the lane, studiously not thinking about anything the entire way. She especially didn't jump at every night sound she heard en route. Or at least that was the story and she planned to stick to it. But when she reached her house, her heart sank yet again. It was as brightly lit as Jet's had been, and Isaiah stood sentry on the front porch. The moment she stepped onto the lawn and held up a hand in greeting, he yelled, "It's okay. She's home."

She forced a smile, but her shoulders immediately developed a defeated slump. Not only had she not managed to save her brother, but now she was going to get grounded from her workshop until she was twenty. It was the worst punishment she could think of other than being forced to attend etiquette and deportment with the other girls in her class. Ugh. With her luck, she'd end up with both punishments.

Isaiah came running out onto the lawn, and she braced herself for the inevitable series of questions and demands to know where she'd been and whether or not she'd been thinking about the fact that she was giving everybody heart attacks. It didn't happen. Instead, he hugged her so hard her back cracked. She couldn't think of the last time one of her brothers had hugged her voluntarily. It made her immediately wonder who had died.

But then he said, "Sal, we were worried sick," and she felt a mixed wave of guilt and relief.

"I'm sorry," she said, her voice weak because he was squeezing all of the air out of her lungs. "I didn't mean to frighten everybody."

Then she found herself in the middle of a cluster of brothers, all determined to embrace her and see for themselves that she was okay.

Even Henry managed to hug her without trying to put anything living into her hair or down the back of her shirt. But still, none of them pressed her for answers about where she'd been or what she'd been thinking. The lack of questions was starting to unnerve her.

Then a pair of soft arms went around her from behind, and Ma turned her around and pulled her close. Her mother smelled like baby powder and cookies and home. Sally finally relaxed and found herself talking. She was going to tell the truth, minus the scariest bits because why frighten her mother unnecessarily. If Ma still refused to believe her, at least she'd know that she had tried.

"I'm sorry if I scared you, Ma. But I knew that if I came to find you, it would be too late to help James. He really was in trouble. I swear I'm not lying."

"Hush, baby," Ma said, brushing her hair back from her forehead with a warm hand. "The boys told me all about those vile moneylenders. I didn't believe them at first until they showed me the note on his bed, and then I was plumb worried sick. We sent a wire to the police in Chicago, and they said they'd send their best man in. I forget the name...John, what was the name again?"

"It was James...James Lotus or something like that," said John from his spot at Ma's elbow. He held the sleeping baby in the crook of his arm.

"The Jade Lotus." Sally smiled as the pieces clicked together. "It's not a man, Ma. I think they're like a Chinatown police squad or something. I'm glad you called them. They showed up just in time. Thanks."

"Come on in and have some supper. You must be famished." Ma wiped her hands briskly on her apron and gestured to the rest of the boys. "And the rest of you shoo. She's home and she's safe, but she doesn't need all of you rabble hovering over her shoulder while she has some grub. All of you get to bed now, and no funny business tonight. My poor heart can't take any more fuss."

To Sally's surprise, they didn't put up any fuss at all. It was like her normally defiant brothers had been replaced with well-behaved alien clones while she was gone. It was too bad she'd missed the aliens. If she'd gotten home in time to see them, she would have thanked them repeatedly for civilizing her brothers and then tried to reverse engineer their space ship.

One by one, they chucked Sally on the shoulder—they must have been spending time with Mr. Black—or gave her a one-armed brother-hug complete with back thump, and bid her good night. John took the baby to his bassinet. Then they tromped up the stairs with a relatively small amount of shoving and head rubs, followed by the slamming of bedroom doors.

Ma led Sally into the kitchen, shaking her head. "Those boys," she said. "Thank the lord in heaven for you, because I don't know what I would do without at least one girl to keep me sane."

Sally looked down at her dingy clothes and black rimmed finger-nails and sighed as Ma began assembling a heavenly-smelling dinner from a series of towel-covered bowls. "I'm not sure I'm doing much good to you in the girly department, Ma."

"Why on earth would you say that?"

"I don't wear dresses except for when I have to. I can't cook very well. Ralphie could probably mend better than me, and I'm not... sometimes I think I'm not the family type, Ma. I understand machines much more than people. It's like my girl setting is broken."

"Oh, pish." Ma set Sally's plate on the table and paused to set her hand on her daughter's shoulder before going to the icebox for the milk. "There's a reason you were the one who hared off to Chicago to rescue your brother, and it wasn't just because you were the first to find the note. It's because of who you are, little chick, and your Ma is proud of you whether you wear dresses or overalls or both at once."

Laughing and tearing up all at once, Sally choked a little on her biscuit. And this time, it wasn't because it was burnt and inedible.

"Now, as for your brother..." Ma added ominously. "He's going to feel the long end of my spoon sure enough. Didn't we teach him better than to get involved with a bunch of lowlife moneylenders? I'm sure we did. Where is he now?"

"He chose not to come home," Sally mumbled. "I tried to get him to, but he chose the bad guys over me, even after everything they did. I wanted to bring him home, Ma. I really tried." And now the tears really did come, because James's betrayal hurt more than she cared to admit. She would have chosen family over just about anything, but he'd thrown her over without blinking an eye.

"That boy will come to no good. No woman wants to say that about her flesh and blood, and it pains me to no end, but that doesn't change what's true. But you, Sally, are going to do wonderful things." Ma rubbed Sally's back while she cried into her plate, and eventually the sniffles died away. "Don't you fret over this, now. He makes his own choices, and that's no reflection on you. You keep on doing what you do best, you hear me?"

Sally nodded. She knew exactly where to start. First thing tomorrow morning. Whatever happened next, she'd be prepared for it. Because even though she was hoping with every ounce of her being that this was over...maybe it wasn't. There was no way to know what to expect, especially with at least two crazy men in the equation. She was counting Doktor Proktor and the Steel Don in that category. Maybe even James, but she wasn't sure about that.

"And the next time you have a problem, I promise I'll listen better." Ma took a deep breath. "I'll admit I was plumb mad when I heard you'd gone, but then I sat myself down and thought things out. I can't say that if I'd been in your shoes I would have done anything different.

You didn't have anyone to turn to, and I'm sorry for that. Things have been tough around here, especially with Pa away at the auction, and me taking care of Ralphie while he's sick. You've had to take on a lot. But it'll get better soon. It has to."

Sally nodded again. Despite her best efforts, the long day was getting to her. She kept jerking herself upright in a losing effort to avoid falling asleep in her potatoes. The plate clattered as Ma cleared the table, and then she gave up the fight. The last thing she remembered was thinking that the table was awful comfortable, and then she fell asleep with her head pillowed on her arms.

CHAPTER 17

The next day, Sally spent most of the morning trying to stretch the crick out of her neck. Ma must have put her to bed at some point during the night, because that's where she'd woken up, but she'd still ended up with a restless sleep and sore muscles. Maybe she was feeling the aftereffects of the overloaded bomb?

Either way, she found it tough to sit still during lessons despite her intentions to be a model student just this once. Her jitters didn't go unnoticed. The other girls, perfect in their starched dresses and lace collars, laughed behind their hands while she squirmed and pinched herself in an effort to stay awake and mobile. Eugene Falks, recovered from his quack attack and holding a grudge over it, kept jabbing her sore spots with the end of his pencil. The chaos didn't go unnoticed, and of course she took the blame for it despite her protests. Miss Cranston set her to clapping erasers after school. Sally hated doing the erasers, especially the way the chalk got all over the front of her hated school dress. It would need a good washing, and she didn't want to waste a minute that could be better spent working on the metal man.

Jet had waited for her while she was getting all over chalk, and this time she came outside to find him and only him. No crazy Syndicate men with scars on their faces. No bullies with ham fists. Just Jet. His bruises were already starting to go yellow, and after the fuss his dad had put up over them, he wore them with pride.

They walked to her workshop together in comfortable silence. He'd risked his life for her and vice versa—what else needed saying? It felt like the beginning of something big and safe and awesome, the kind of partnership that Calamity Sue and Jet Blackwood would have dreamt of, if only they were real people.

It was a warm spring day. Yellow pollen rimmed the edges of the road, and daffodils poked their bobbing heads up toward the sun. They passed farmers laying seed in the fields, and Kly the mailman attempting to lead his horse away from a field of clover, and a motorcar parked randomly alongside the lane. Sally's heart leapt at the sight, expecting to see Frankie Ratchet emerge once again with a gun and a job offer, but it was empty. No one would shoot at them today—that's what she told herself to quell the nervousness. Maybe she even believed it. Why would they, when no one in the Steel Syndicate knew the real robot still sat in her workshop? They all thought it had been destroyed, so she could take all the time in the world to tinker, to take it apart, to feel her way through the map of its insides. She could hardly wait.

By the time Jet pushed open the workshop door, she was unable to restrain the excited giggles. Then he started laughing at her, and instead of getting angry she just laughed harder. It felt like a weight had been lifted from her. She drew the tarp off the robot with a flourish and posed dramatically.

"Bravo!" Jet said, clapping. "I've never seen anyone take a blanket off something with such style."

She threw it at him, and he ducked, and they spent a few minutes chasing each other around the workshop. She threw hay into his hair, and he retaliated by tackling her and tickling until she worried she might burst. Finally, she called for a truce, because she couldn't wait another minute to take apart the robot.

After the first half hour or so, she managed to stop squealing, but it was tough. She'd never seen anything like BEM before in her life. Doktor Proktor may have been a crazy scientist, but he was a *genius* crazy scientist, and that had to count for something. The only unfortunate part of the whole thing was that some essential bits in the torso had been destroyed when those Syndicate yahoos shot it. Disgusted, she tossed her wrench down in the dirt and sat down with an exasperated huff.

Jet was at her side in a second. He'd been watching from the loft; she had no idea how he'd gotten down so quickly unless he'd jumped. He'd always loved heights. She didn't get that one bit. She wasn't a chicken, but heights sometimes gave her a dizzy, queasy feeling in the pit of her stomach.

"What?" he demanded. "What's wrong?"

She hung her head. "This part—I'm calling it the Moveaton—is broken. That mangled Square Power Thingy is cracked, and I can't generate any air pressure without it." From the way she spoke, you could hear the capital letters. It had always been a talent of hers. A completely useless talent, but a talent nonetheless.

He ran a hand through his hair, which was already corkscrewed into more directions than it should have been and still had a few pieces of hay in it. "Can't you make another one? You're good at building things."

"Thanks for the vote of confidence, but I don't think so. This is the kind of craftsmanship you can't just slap together with a couple of old tools and some scrap metal. I'd need to forge the pieces, and there's pressure levels to consider…" His eyes had started to glaze over already; usually it took at least three or four sentences before that happened.

He wasn't so interested in the technical stuff despite her best efforts to show him how interesting it really was. So she sighed and went for the simple explanation: "Look, if I mess it up, the whole thing could go kaboom."

"Oooooh!" He drew the word into one long, approving sound. "I getcha."

She heard a voice then, coming from directly over her shoulder. The voice was thready and faint, which made it tough to recognize. Actually, it was hard to place as male or female; that's how quiet it was.

It said something that sounded like "power backup."

She grabbed the wrench off the ground and whirled around to face whoever had snuck into her workshop, but there was no one there. The corner in question was empty save for a lone crate of spare bolts and scrap she'd begged off of Mr. Black the last time she'd helped out in his garage. But there was no way anyone could hide behind that unless they'd been hit by a shrink ray. Since stranger things had happened in the recent past, she checked. No midgets.

Jet was looking at her funny. "What are you doing?" he asked.

"Didn't you hear that? The thing about the backup power source." She looked around the room but saw no one. "Who's there?" she asked. Still no response, and now that she thought to look, there were no footprints on the dirt floor other than hers and Jet's.

"I didn't hear anything," he said.

"Check the loft," she said. He looked at her skeptically, clearly expecting her to bust out in laughter because the whole thing was a joke. But he climbed the ladder when she failed to deliver.

"What am I looking for, exactly?" he called down to her.

"An intruder. Someone was here; I swear it. I don't know how you didn't hear them. Have you cleaned out your ears lately?"

Jet held up a handful of hay with a threat in his eyes, and she immediately apologized because the last thing she needed was a broken robot full of dried grass.

"Sorry," she said. "Just joking."

He grinned and relaxed. "Sure you were."

Then he started rummaging around in the loft. She used the space to store her inventions, so it was incredibly cluttered. A still-in-progress milking machine leaned up against a crate full of failed bottle warming contraptions. Jet weaved around that but managed to trip over the vacuum tubes of the Hair Trimmificater, which had worked a little too well and was banished to the loft after she'd made Carl half bald.

And those were just a small portion of the strange things stashed up in the loft. It was a lot for one person to search through on their own, but she didn't want to climb up there and risk the intruder escaping out the door before they had a chance to question him. Or her. Or it.

Even though she knew there was a ton of space to search and he'd tell her the moment he found anything, it was still hard to restrain her impatience. "Find anything?" she called.

"Just hold your horses!" he shot back.

She threw up her hands and turned back to the robot, thinking that maybe she'd take a quick look for this mysterious power source, in case that voice had been telling the truth. The strangest sight greeted her. A violet haze hung in the air over the robot. It had the wispy look of fog, only tinted a bright and vibrant purple. She'd seen colored smoke before, but this smoke held a shape—an irregular oval about the size of Ma's favorite serving platter. That struck Sally as impossible.

Not half as impossible as when she heard that faint, whispering voice again and swore it was coming from the mist.

"The base of the torso."

She had to be imagining it. A floating mist that talked? All the stress of the past few days had gotten to her, and there was no shame in that. But she didn't want to admit it to Jet until she was certain that this wasn't really happening, and the only way to be certain was to look and see if the voice was right. So she grabbed her trusty wrench and set to work loosening the bolts where the robot's torso met the legs. It was a strange place to put a backup power source. She knew it wouldn't be there.

But it was. As soon as she pried the curled metal off the robot's hips, she saw an intact cube, smaller but of the same design as the broken piece she'd named the Square Power Thingy. And now that she saw it, she had to admit the design was a smart move. It was an ideal location for a power source, with easy access to the lower limbs and a thick, protective metal covering. It was only a matter of reconnecting it like so and then she would theoretically be able to power the machine back up. There was still the broken Moveaton to deal with, but...

It was a terrific breakthrough, but it also meant that she wasn't hallucinating. There was a cloud in her workshop, and it was talking to her. As if things couldn't get any weirder than they already had.

CHAPTER 18

"Hey, Jet?" Sally said. Her voice sounded funny to her own ears, high pitched and uncertain. And if Sally Slick knew anything, it was how to lay down the law to anyone listening. "Could you come down here? A purple fog is talking to me, and I'm not really sure how to handle it."

He snorted. It seemed like a waste of breath to tell him she was serious, because why would he believe her? He'd just have to see for himself, and then they could talk.

The rickety ladder leading to the loft shook alarmingly as he made his way halfway down it and then jumped the rest of the way to the ground, landing in a neat crouch. He straightened, looking around briskly. "All right," he said, "what's this talking fog thing about? It's a joke, right?"

"No." She pointed at the foggy apparition, which still hovered over the open robot. "It's right there. Are you blind?"

He squinted in that direction and then moved a step to the side as if a better viewpoint might help him see what she was talking about.

His forehead furrowed with worry. She knew what he was going to say before his mouth even opened.

"Sal, I'm sorry. I don't see anything."

Dimly, she heard the voice again, but she didn't stop to listen this time. Jet *had* to believe her. They'd always been a team, and she couldn't stand the thought that he might give up on her as a complete loonybin.

"Look," she said. "Look at the robot. The fog told me there was a spare power source, and it's here. Right here. If I was just hallucinating, it wouldn't be there, right?"

"Riiiight. Unless it's something you knew but didn't know you knew, so you had to imagine a purple fog to tell yourself what you know."

Sally blinked. "I think that's actually crazier than the idea that there's a talking purple fog in the room right now."

He snorted again. "Yeah."

The fog drifted toward Sally, its edges roiling in what looked like agitation. It suddenly seemed like a very bad idea to anger the talking fog. She backed up an involuntary step, lifting her hands like she might ward off a punch. From fog. As stupid as she knew this was, she couldn't exactly help herself.

"Sally, what's going on?" Jet asked. "You're worrying me."

She would have answered, but the fog spoke again, and this time she listened. "The Visionator," it said.

"That's it!" she exclaimed. "The Visionator! The Doktor hit me with that Visionator, and the beam was purple, right? Well, this... cloud thing? It's the same color."

"Soooo...?" Jet frowned thoughtfully.

"So the Visionator allows me to see and interact with..."

Jet added brightly, "Things that are purple?" just as the fog said something.

"Shut up!" she hissed. "Say that again, fog."

"Ghosts," it whispered, drifting closer. "I'm a ghost."

"Oh." She looked up at it, nodding like ghostly apparitions in her workshop were an everyday kind of thing. "Sure. A ghost."

Then she fainted.

When she came to on the floor of the workshop, surrounded by stray tools and bits of straw, Jet was dabbing at her forehead with a damp cloth. That was a nice gesture except that she knew all the cloths in the workshop had been used to wipe grease off her hands at one time or another. She batted his hand away and sat up.

"Are you okay?" he asked worriedly.

"Of course I am," she said. "I think I must just be hungry. Got a little woozy there."

"Yeah. Sure."

They stared at each other, but neither of them brought up the fog or dared to suggest that she might have fainted over that whole ghost situation. In fact, if Sally had her way, the whole thing would be wiped from their memories forever. Too bad she couldn't invent something that would make it happen. Although there were possibilities...

But her plate was already pretty full, what with the robot and the Syndicate and the ghostly apparition. She still couldn't believe it herself. Apparently, that Jade Lotus man hadn't been kidding when he'd said there was magic involved here. She pushed herself up to standing and looked around. There was no purple haze hanging anywhere around the workshop as far as she could see, and the disappointed feeling in the pit of her stomach was more than a little surprising.

"Where did it go?" she asked. "The ghost?"

"Here." Jet handed her a slightly smushed sandwich from his backpack, and she stared at it like she was wondering what she was supposed to do with it. "You said you were hungry."

"Oh. Yeah." She shoved half of it into her mouth, practically gluing her jaws together. Surprisingly, she found that she really was hungry, even though she'd just been making an excuse so she didn't feel so silly for having fainted. "Suh whuhsh da guh?"

"I have no idea what you're saying to me right now."

She swallowed. "So where's the ghost?"

"Oh. I told it to go out of the room for a little while. Did it listen?"

A wave of gratitude rushed over Sally. He might not believe her, but he'd still made the effort to cover her back just in case. She couldn't have asked for a better best friend, but that kind of gushing was embarrassing, so she limited herself to smiling at him. "Yeah. Help me up, will ya?" After he helped her to her feet, she went to the door and opened it. To her relief, the violet cloud hung right outside the shop. "Hey, ghost guy? Come on in."

To her intense surprise, the ghost took her invitation literally. It swooped down toward her body and straight into her open mouth. There was a strange sense of vertigo, and then she got shoved off into the corner of her own head. She could still see and hear, but when she tried to say something, nothing happened. She tried to move her arm. Nothing. It was a little panic inducing, to be entirely honest.

She felt her mouth move, but the voice that came out wasn't her own. It was male, for starters, with the kind of rasp that comes with a bad cold or an overzealous smoking habit. And it had the kind of jaunt to it that suggested a bounce in his step. The kind of guy who talks a big talk and isn't afraid of nothing.

It said, "They call me the Creep."

Jet looked alarmed. "Sally? Are you okay? Your eyes are purple."

"The little missy? She's fine," said the Creep. "She's just letting me borrow her mouth for a minute, and then I'll hit the road, Jack. You get it?" At Jet's blank look, he sighed. "No one ever gets my jokes."

"Prove that Sally's okay," Jet challenged.

"She's fine. And I'm gonna tell her how to fix that robot over there as payment for this here loan of her mouth, okay? You okay with that, missy?"

Sally, feeling more than a little disoriented and confused by what was happening, tried to speak, but still couldn't manage it. So she thought as hard as she could: *"Sure."* Because what else was she supposed to say? She didn't like feeling like a passenger in her own body at all, but she also wasn't going to rest until she figured out what was going on with the ghost. It wasn't the kind of thing you could just dismiss. And having some help with the robot would be awfully nice too.

"She says yes," said the Creep. "Now are you going to let me say what I need to say here, kid? Because we don't have much time."

"All right." Jet perched on Calamity's running board, his arms folded and lips turned down in a scowl. The posture would have looked very forbidding on someone else, but on his gawky frame, it just reminded Sally of a very irate chicken. "Make it quick," Jet said. "And if Sally's hurt, you and I are going to have some words."

The Creep snickered. "All right, Tough Guy. I promise not to hurt her. Now listen good, because here's the scoop. I worked for the Steel Syndicate when I was alive. I have...skills, y' see? I can get things for you if you pay the price, things that are locked up tight."

"So you're a thief."

"I *was* a thief. Yeah. I was one of the best in Chicago. They called me the Creep because I could get in and out without anyone hearing a thing. Just as quiet as a mouse."

"If you were that good, what happened?"

"The Steel Don happened, that's what. The man's a complete nutcase. He said I stole from him, and I didn't do nothing like that. Why would I steal from the boss? I'm not the kind of dummy who bites the hand that feeds him, I'll tell you that. So he says I stole his stuff, and I say no sirree, and then I find myself off the pier with a bullet in my back."

"That's...that's terrible."

"No kidding! The louse says he's going to go after my wife and kids too, after I didn't do nuffink. It was all that Proktor guy. He was the one grifting equipment, and we all tried to tell the Don, but he don't listen to us. So after I died, I decided to stick around to protect my wife and kids. The Don hasn't gone after 'em yet, because he was all distracted by the two of you."

"But they can't see you, right?"

"Exactly. The only one who can see me now is Proktor, and I'll be darned if I go to him for help after he's the one who got me whacked in the first place. But I followed him, since I was worried about my wife and kids. Once he hit your girl here with the Visionator, I decided I might see if you'd be willing to make a trade."

"What's that?" Jet sounded cautious, his eyes searching Sally's purple ones.

"I'll help you if you help me get a message to my wife and kids. They got to get out of Dodge before he comes after 'em. Will you help me? You gotta answer quick."

"Oh, that's all? Of course I'll do that." Jet didn't even hesitate. "I don't agree with stealing, but threatening little kids is just plain wrong. But I don't see why we need your help, mister. The Steel Don is done with us. James is gone with Doktor Proktor, and for all the Syndicate knows, we blew up the real robot in the Golden Pagoda. There isn't anything they could want from us now."

"*Au contrairey*, my friend," said the ghost, sounding more like a country bumpkin than a Frenchman. "The Steel Don wants one thing from you now, and that's revenge. And he's on his way here to get it. Like *now*."

CHAPTER 19

Sally couldn't believe the words that were coming out of her mouth, probably because her mouth was currently being possessed by a ghost. The Steel Don wanted revenge? She found it very difficult to believe that the head of a major crime syndicate would bother with vengeance on a couple of teenagers, even if they *had* blown up one of his hideouts. She'd been worried he might figure out that she still had BEM-1 and come back for that, but viewing them as a threat to his crime mob? That was ridiculous.

Jet was on the same wavelength as her. He didn't look particularly alarmed either, mostly disbelieving. "No way," he said. "He has no reason to come here again. We didn't do anything wrong."

"You made him look bad when he's trying real hard to bring all the criminals under his rule, kid. If he doesn't take you and the little missy down, he looks like a sap who can't even handle a couple munchkins. He gots to make an example of you if he wants to make this deal happen. So it's just business. Well, that and the fact that he's a crazy man who can't stand the fact that you made him look even worse than that spooky metal face of his."

"So he's coming to..." Jet couldn't finish the sentence.

"Kill you," the ghost said. "I left Chi-town when they did, but I travels a lot faster than them on account of the fact that I can fly through things. They'll be here in the next half hour or so. That's why I says you have to choose fast."

"Why didn't you say that in the first place?" demanded Jet, his eyes wild.

Sally felt her shoulders shrug. "I didn't want to influence your decision, eh? You got to come to these things on your own terms."

"My own terms? They're going to kill us!" Jet began to pace quickly back and forth. "Okay, here's what we do. Sally, you get your family and take them to my house. My pa will help look after your ma and the baby. I'll go get Sheriff Brownlee."

"Your Sherriff wouldn't last two ticks against the Syndicate men. They shoots first and asks questions later."

"But...then...what do we do? We can't just give up. They might shoot us!"

"I need a body," the ghost said thoughtfully. "If I had a body, I could make a stand while you two escaped, and then I could get my wife and girls to safety."

"Sure." Jet threw up his hands. "We'll just run down to the corner shop and buy you one. Easy peasy."

Sally's head swiveled to look around the room, and she and the Creep had the same idea at the same time.

The robot! she exclaimed silently, her voice echoing in her own mind.

"The robot!" the ghost said aloud. Then he chuckled. "Nice thinking, missy."

"What?" Jet frowned. "I didn't say anything."

"I was talking to your girlfriend."

Jet turned red from the tips of his ears all the way down into his collar, the kind of bright beet red you can't pretend to miss. He shuffled his feet and mumbled something under his breath that could have been "She's not my girlfriend," or maybe "Sails got your errand." Sally wasn't quite sure, and she didn't have control of her own body, so she couldn't ask. It was probably better that way. As a whole, all the girlfriend-boyfriend lovey-dovey stuff made her twitch. It seemed like such a waste of time to sit around mooning over some boy when there were so many cool things to do and see. It was good that she and Jet had the same priorities when it came to that kind of thing.

"What do you say, missy?" asked the ghost. "If I pops out of here, do you think we could get this metal monster up and moving so I can take it for a ride?"

A wave of uncertainty rushed over her. Sally wasn't used to feeling nervous like this when it came to machines, but there was so much at stake. With her usual inventions, an error meant she might have to rethink the design, or possibly scrounge for enough metal to jury rig a new part. But now? A mistake on her part could mean death.

But what other choice did she have? It was just like the problems with Eugene; they only got worse if you hid your head in the sand and did nothing.

I'll try, she thought. *But you've got to get out of my body and let me work.*

"Done," said the Creep.

Sally's mouth opened, and out poured the purple ghostly haze. Her awareness slid back into her body, her muscles once again under her control. She felt super aware of how it felt to move her hand, lick her lips, take in a breath and let it out. It felt like waking up from a long fever, where everything was unreal and disjointed. Jet watched her face, his head tilted to one side.

"Coooool," he breathed. "Is that you, Sally? The purple just drained out of your eyes like water from a leaky bucket."

"Very poetic, Jet," she said, and the voice that came out of her mouth was her own. Before she could stop herself, she let out a little squeal of excitement. That whole possession thing had been pretty interesting, but she didn't care to repeat it any time soon. Funny how you could miss your own voice.

Jet must have missed it too, because he let out a whoop and then clapped a hand over his mouth like that sound was the secret Syndicate mating call and might attract some unwanted attention. She couldn't help it. She snickered. Behind her, she could hear the faint echo of the Creep laughing along with her.

He lowered his hands and gave her a sheepish grin. "So you're fixing the robot. What do I do?"

"I need you to convince my ma to take Ralphie over to visit with your ma, then start fortifying the exits."

He nodded, took two steps toward the door, and then stopped. "We're going to barricade ourselves in here? Isn't that a losing proposition?" He paused, his face going pale as a fearful thought occurred to him. "You're not going to blow up the barn, are you? Your pa would throw a hissy."

"Don't be silly," she said, too distracted to be offended. "We want a safe location to fall back on, that's all."

Sally climbed the ladder to the loft with Jet at her heels and took a long look at the various inventions piled about. She'd intended them to be useful, to make the tedious jobs of everyday farm life a little more fun. But now she was looking at them with a new set of eyes, and they weren't the ghost's. These were the eyes of a girl who knew the safety of her family was at stake. Those Syndicate boys wouldn't know what hit them.

"Jet, we're in a barn with a robot, a racing tractor, and umpteen Sally Slick inventions. Do you really think blowing up the barn is the best I can do?"

She looked down at him, and whatever was on her face must have been pretty serious indeed, because he took a step back. Then the fear melted from his face, and he nodded. In that moment, he looked much older than fourteen. He looked like a shorter version of the man she knew he'd eventually become, a man who stood up against impossible odds because someone had to do it, one who shot for the sky. Sally had no idea what was going to happen to them once the Steel Syndicate arrived, but she knew one thing—Jet Black would never be bullied again.

She gave him a quick, impulsive hug. He stiffened like she'd spit on him, and she punched him in the shoulder. They broke out into laughter that was only half strained, and Sally felt like she should punch *herself* in the shoulder if only it were physically possible to do so. After all this time struggling against the urge, what had she been thinking to hug Jet like that? It ventured way too close to the aforementioned lovey-dovey stuff. It was the kind of thing best friends simply did not do.

She cleared her throat. "We should probably get moving. We don't have much time."

"Yeah." He shifted from foot to foot and seemed about to say something. "I'll just get to work then."

"Okay."

He turned lightly on one foot, quickly descended the ladder, and whistled his way out the door. Anyone looking at him would think he was without a care in the world, but Sally knew it was an act. Jet didn't whistle when he was in a good mood. He hummed.

Either way, if Ma was at home, Sally didn't doubt that Jet would be able to charm her into visiting his house. Their mothers liked to chat over a cup of tea sometimes. Once, Sally had heard them trying to make a match between her and Jet. Her face went scarlet in remembered mortification, but only the ghost was there to see it.

"Ooooh," the Creep teased in his faint voice. "Sally and Jeeeet... kissing in a tree!" It would have continued the song except that she took her favorite wrench and flung it with expert aim right through the heart of its purple cloud. "Hey! That wasn't keen at all!"

"Then stop singing and help me figure this thing out." She wiped sweaty palms on the legs of her overalls and walked toward the robot. "I should be able to hook up the secondary power without a problem, but there's still the issue of this Moveaton thing here. Without it, I don't think we can make it walk."

The violet glow drifted closer as she pointed. "I don't know much about machine type stuff," he said. "But I did catch a glimpse of Proktor's diagrams once. If you get something to write with, I can tell you what the insides looked like before some sap filled it with lead."

"No way. How are you going to remember all that?"

The glow brightened considerably, and the Creep's answering whisper was filled with pride. "Photographic memory, toots. That's what made me the best creep in town. I could study a layout once and commit it to memory. Never needed to carry a map or nothing."

"That's...impressive." Sally pulled out a screwdriver and squatted down in the dirt. "I don't have the time to go inside for a pen, so this'll have to do. Teach me how to make a robot, Creepy."

"It's the Creep." The ghost sighed. "No Y."

"That's what you get for calling me 'toots.'"

She heard a faint snort and would have responded, but the Creep started giving her directions, and the tip of the screwdriver scratched faint lines in the dirt. The lines became boxes. The boxes became systems, and her mind filled with the all-consuming excitement that came with bringing an invention to life.

CHAPTER 20

The Syndicate arrived five minutes later than expected, but Sally wasn't about to complain. The Creep had stationed himself out in the yard; Jet attempted to nail boards to the doors without impaling his thumb, and Sally tried to keep from snatching the hammer from him and showing him how to use it correctly. Improper tool usage made her twitch. But she had so much left to do; she'd have to give him a class on how to handle a hammer later.

She was loosening the bolts on Calamity's new air-cooled turbo propulsion system for the fifth time when the Creep flew in through the open loft.

"Here they come," he hissed. "Is my body ready?"

"The robot's operational, but be careful. That right leg joint sticks, and you're going to have a hard time getting up if you fall over. But this new engine won't stay on Calamity," she said, scowling. "I need more time."

"You don't have it."

"Then we're toast." She selected a new bolt, tightening it with furious, rapid strokes. "The harness isn't tight enough; the engine keeps falling off. Two more minutes, and I can make it work."

"Sally Slick!" The shout came from outside. It was loud and masculine and it meant business. "Come out of the barn. Now."

"Who is that?" she yelled, still working furiously.

"The Steel Don. We have something to discuss. Come out now."

"I don't have anything to say to you!"

She hefted the propulsion system into place on the back of the tractor, staggering slightly under the weight. The straps were just a couple inches too short, and she didn't have enough time to make new ones. The whole thing fell to the ground with a clang, smashing her foot. A muffled swear word escaped her lips, the kind of word Pa said when he dropped things and then made her and her brothers promise never to repeat.

"What was that?" the Steel Don shouted. He sounded angry. "What did you say to me?"

"I didn't say anything to you. I smashed my foot!"

"You lie!"

She threw up her hands in exasperation, not like he could see her through the wall. But really, she had no idea how this guy could run an entire crime syndicate. He was more over-sensitive than Miss Cranston, and she took offense at everything.

"Never mind," she said in a quieter voice. "It's not worth trying to reason with this guy, is it?"

"No," said the Creep. "He has to take offense. He has to prove his dominance over you. Nothing you can say is going to change that."

"Fine. Take the robot; let's see how it works."

The Creep didn't wait for a second. His purple glow swept toward the prone form of the robot. There was a long moment while Sally waited breathlessly for the creak of metal in motion. Instead, she heard the rattle of wood as someone outside checked the front door, and the muffled murmur of voices discussing the best way to get inside and capture "those pesky kids." It sounded like they were outnumbered. By a lot.

While she was distracted by the men outside, the robot sat up. Its eyes glowed purple, and it moved without a signal from the control device. She heard a muffled sound as it ponderously swung its legs off the table, like someone talking with their lips glued shut. The Creep was trying to talk, but the machine's mouth didn't move.

"I can't understand you," she said. "I'll have to make you a mouth later."

He made a muffled noise that was probably a yes. Then he nodded.

The door rattled again, harder this time, and then there was a thump as someone struck it. Dust rained down from the ceiling, but Jet's bent-nailed boards held. The robot ponderously crossed the room with a tilted, uneven gait due to the bad joint on one side. But it stayed upright, so that was something. The Creep lifted his metal arms to brace the door. This time, when the men struck it, it barely moved. Even though his robot face couldn't change expression, Sally had the strange feeling that he was grinning on the inside.

BAM!

The robot may have been immobile, but Sally could see that the door wouldn't last forever. The wood was old and warped with age; even the thickest planks couldn't stand up against this kind of a beating for long. And if the Syndicate men realized there was a back door, they'd be captured even quicker. They had to get out, but without Calamity's new turbo propulsion system, her escape plan wasn't going to work. She'd originally planned to send the robot out first to draw their pursuit, and while the mob men were cowering before him, she and Jet could have made their escape on Calamity—or at least they could have if the new propulsion engine was in place. Their brilliant plan seemed doomed to fail, and Sally was frightened.

Jet seemed to share her nervousness. He climbed hurriedly down the first few rungs of the ladder and then leapt the rest of the way to the ground.

"What do we do?" he demanded. "Do we make a rush for it on foot? Or do we ride Calamity and hope for the best?"

She thought about it. The racing tractor was fast enough to win a race, but not to outrun a bullet. With the new propulsion system, Calamity would have had enough get up and go to make their escape. But without the extra engine? She didn't think it was a bet worth making.

"I don't know," she said, trying in vain not to feel ashamed. Her one plan had failed, and she couldn't come up with a second, and the men wouldn't stop banging. "I just don't know. We could attack them with some of these...?"

She gestured toward the pile of her inventions, which had seemed like insurmountable weapons just half an hour earlier. But now they seemed like a terrible risk. Could she really look a man in the eye and bean him with the Seed Planter? It was heavy enough to knock someone cold, but what if she missed? And could she strike fast enough to get them through safely? The inventions could be weapons in the right hands, sure, but she wasn't a brawler. She'd learned to take care of herself well enough as the lone girl in a family of brothers, but that wasn't the same as taking on a bunch of gangsters with guns singlehandedly, was it?

Her eyes began to fill with helpless, angry tears. For all her so-called potential, for all the talent, she sure was stupid. When she'd heard the Syndicate was coming, why didn't she insist they hide? Because of what the Creep had said? But he didn't have anything to lose and everything to gain. He wasn't exactly an unbiased counselor. She'd listened to him anyway, because he was telling her things she wanted to hear. He was playing into this whole picture she had of herself as someone who was special, someone destined to do great things, and she'd thought that meant she was pretty invincible because how could she do great things if she was dead? Now she realized how wrong she'd been, and it was going to get her and Jet killed.

She heard Jet moving about behind her, the scuff of his shoes in the dirt accompanied by a rustle of movement. Then the silence was broken by another strike on the door.

BANG!

Dust motes and straw rained down on her from the loft. They could hide up there, maybe even pull the ladder up, but it would only delay the inevitable. They'd be captured. Or maybe the gang would just shoot them and leave. Up in the loft, they'd be like ducks in a barrel. Or whatever that saying was.

She kept waiting for Jet to come and hug her, or maybe to hit her upside the head for being such an idiot and getting them both killed, but he didn't. He just kept moving around behind her as the bad guys continued to break down the door. Probably pacing. That was it. He was scared, and he hated her too much to want to hug her at the end.

"Come on," he muttered. "We don't have much time."

She turned to look at him without bothering to wipe her face. Let him see her cry. Let him see how terrible she felt, because her ego had killed him, and he just didn't know he was dead yet. But when she lifted her blurry eyes to look at him, what she saw made her blink. The two remaining tears poured down her cheeks, clearing her vision.

He was wearing the propulsion engine on his back. The harness she'd manufactured out of metal, the one that had been just a bit too small to attach to the tractor, had been tightened with a sturdy length of nylon strapping that crisscrossed his chest. It fit him better than it had the tractor, almost like she'd made it for him without even realizing what she was doing. Still, the thing was hefty. As she watched, he staggered a little under the weight and then shifted it on his back with a wince.

"Jet," she said cautiously, "what are you doing?"

"I'm getting us out of here," he said. "What else would I be doing?"

"But... Look, it's a nice thought, but the minute you turn that thing on, you're going to shoot right up into the sky. It's meant to propel big, heavy stuff, Jet. On something as light as you? It'll fly."

"Exactly." He bounced on his toes exactly once before he listed to the side and almost fell over. "Whoops. This thing is pretty hard to manage, but I figure once I turn it on, it'll be much easier to maneuver."

"Don't be ridic..." she began to scoff, but the more she thought about it, maybe it wasn't such a half bad idea after all. They could zoom out of the barn and hide somewhere. The Steel Don couldn't stay here forever looking for them. Eventually he'd realize they weren't worth it, especially when the Creep stomped out in his robot body and went to save his family. They'd realize they had bigger fish to fry. They'd go away for good this time. Maybe if Sally and Jet had enough time, they could even fake their own deaths. That actually sounded like fun.

"Well? Brilliant, right?" Jet grinned.

"Yeah. Smarter than me. I froze in the face of danger."

He didn't seem disappointed at all. "Hey, that's why we have partners. You've saved my butt plenty of times."

"Please don't talk to me about your butt."

BAM!

The Creep turned his head and made his muffled noises at them again. It didn't take a super genius to figure out what he wanted. He wanted them to quit yakking and hurry up.

"All right," she said, holding out a hand. "Take off the engine and give it to me."

But Jet didn't move. He stood there with a wounded expression on his face. "You don't think I can do it?"

"No, of course not! It's just that..." She was about to say some technical stuff about the operation of the propulsion system and understanding of torque and all the things that could help maneuver the thing in the air, but were they really necessary? Maybe all you needed was the guts to take a leap into the unknown. And if anyone deserved the chance to fly first, it was Jet. He'd come up with the idea. This was his baby now, not hers. "Never mind. You remember how to run it?"

She'd taught him, of course. Jet was her primary audience for product testing. He'd actually driven Calamity once, but only once because the thought of him driving her precious racing tractor into a tree gave Sally the shakes.

"'Course I do! Gimme a second to test it out, and then I'll get us out of here!"

He shifted the straps one last time, thrust one hand up to the sky in a heroic pose, and thumbed the trigger. The engine roared into life, filling the workshop with light and heat and a noise like a billion angry thunder gods. Jet went skyward, dirt billowing in his wake, and crashed straight into the loft.

Sally could barely see, what with all the coughing out dust and wiping dust from her eyes and...well, all the *dust*. She staggered toward the ladder, shouting his name, but she knew it was futile. The engine still roared overhead, blotting out any other noise.

When the man grabbed her from behind, it took her completely by surprise.

He must have figured out that there was a back door and broken in during all the chaos of Jet's takeoff. Strong arms encircled her, lifting her off the ground. She took in a long breath, preparing to scream, but coughed instead.

"I've gotcha, my lassie," the man hissed in her ear. She snuck a peek at him, hoping it was Frankie Ratchet. It wasn't. This man had squinty eyes and bad breath. She recoiled instinctively from the reek.

"Let go!" she exclaimed.

But his hands were like vices. She'd have more luck breaking a length of lead pipe with her hands than she would getting out of this.

Escape would have been impossible if Jet hadn't dropped out of the sky onto the man's head. Between the added weight of the engine and the push of the exhaust, her captor's hands were ripped from her body. The exhaust shoved her across the floor, slamming into the bale of hay Jet sometimes sat on while he watched her work. Her captor wasn't so lucky. He flew into Calamity's side, knocking his head hard against the thick iron. Then he was out like a light...after someone hit it with a hammer.

"Sorry it took me so long," said Jet, staggering over to her under the heavy weight of the engine. "I think I took out your loft."

"Are you okay?" She stood up and began looping the ends of the straps through her overalls and around her waist without wasting any time, thankful that she'd taken the time to change out of her school dress before she'd gotten to work. It wasn't the best effort she'd ever made at a harness, but as long as she held on, she should be safe. She didn't have enough time to manufacture anything better. The last thing she wanted to do was get captured because she was being a perfection-ist. "I mean, that loft is hard, isn't it?"

"It was a good thing I was flying heroically." He held his fist up briefly, then pulled her close. "My hand took most of the damage."

She looked down at the split and bleeding knuckles of the hand wrapped around her waist. Before she could comment on his injury, he pulled the ignition trigger, and they were airborne. Her stomach leapt up into her throat as they soared toward the ceiling on a collision course. Below them, she could see mobsters in black coats and fedoras pouring into the building. The Creep fought them off valiantly, but for every one that his metal arms brought down, two more snuck past him. He just wasn't fast enough, especially with that bum leg.

But they, on the other hand, were *too* fast. They weaved erratically from side to side as Jet attempted to aim for the loft window and the open air beyond. What he lacked in finesse, he made up for in blind luck—they rocketed outside, missing the wall by inches. Sally thought she'd feel less terrified once they were free of any potential obstacles, but soaring straight up into the sky wasn't what she had in mind. They hurtled into the air. The ground grew farther and farther away with every passing second, and only Jet's hands around her waist and a few feet of cord stood between her and splatting on the ground like a squished grape.

Suddenly, breathing became difficult. The air felt weird up here, and her ears felt funny. The noise of the engine became muted. Was it failing? Had they escaped the clutches of the Steel Syndicate only to fall from the sky like Icarus with his melting wings? She'd felt so confident of the invention before, but they'd been on the ground then. Up here, things seemed different. Much more hazardous than they had been in theory.

She panicked, clutching at Jet's arms and hyperventilating until the world swam before her. Faintly, she heard a strange noise from right next to her ear. Jet was laughing.

"This is great!" he whooped. "Look, Sal! Look what happens when I do this!"

He triggered the throttle again, aiming the air stream to one side. Sally had originally designed the propulsion system to help Calamity corner smoothly in the event that they ever raced on a curved track. With their slighter weight and no ground friction, the turning mechanism sent them straight into a corkscrew spin. Her stomach flip-flopped, threatening rebellion. They whirled over and over until the momentum of their rotation threatened to pull Sally right out of Jet's arms.

"Stop!" she shrieked. "Before I fall."

He straightened abruptly, wobbled, flipped upside down, and eventually managed to flip back over right side up. By this time, Sally had squeezed her eyes shut and started taking deep, calming breaths. It would serve those mobsters right if she threw up on their heads, but she didn't want to if she didn't have to.

"All right," he said, seemingly nonplussed by the assorted flips and flops. "Where to?"

"Uh...can I open my eyes now?"

He sounded genuinely confused. "Why'd you close them?"

"Never mind." She cautiously opened one and then the other. The ground beneath them swarmed with men, all pointing up toward them and staring with mouths open in awe. She didn't see any guns aimed in their direction, but it was only a matter of time. The late afternoon sun glinted off the silver face of the Steel Don as he wildly gestured in their direction. Men scattered to obey him before his wrath fell on them instead. She had no idea what he was ordering them to do, but it couldn't be good. "We need to hide."

"We're a little conspicuous up here. We'll have to descend a little and hope to lose them in the trees before we go to ground."

"Do it." She closed her eyes again. "Let me know when it's safe to look again."

"Wimp," he said lightly.

Her stomach swooped, and her ears popped as they took a sharp dive toward the ground. Despite her best intent, she couldn't keep from peeking as the land loomed closer and closer. And closer. And even closer. Men scattered as Jet and Sally bore down on them with blinding speed.

"Jet!" she screamed. "Pull up! Pull up or we'll crash!"

CHAPTER 21

A crash seemed inevitable as they rocketed toward the ground. Sally met the eyes of the Steel Don as they drew closer. His silver mouth curled up in a satisfied smile. It didn't take psychic abilities to know what he was thinking—these troublesome kids would take themselves out of the equation, and that was fine with him.

Then Jet hit the ignition trigger again, cutting the engine. Her belly flip-flopped in fear, and she screamed wordlessly. The ground loomed below them; the collision was only moments away. But instead he twisted in midair, reorienting the rocket, and punched the button again. They took off with a roar a split second before impact, skimming along the ground. Sally felt the sweep of grass under her belly for a few terrifying seconds, and then they began gaining altitude again. If she hadn't been shaking so hard, she would have been impressed. As it was, she concentrated on keeping a good hold on him, because who knew how well the makeshift harness would hold up under all the pressure.

They skimmed over the field and into the bracken, aiming for the woods. Crabgrass whipped Sally's face, drawing blood, but she couldn't bear to loosen her death grip on Jet, not at this speed. Within seconds, they'd left their pursuers behind. Now all they had to worry about was getting impaled on a tree. Sally was pretty sure that heroically sticking her hand out ahead of them like Jet had in the workshop wouldn't be much help at the speed they were going, even if she could have brought herself to do it.

Before she knew it, they were in the trees. Jet seemed to know exactly what to do, shifting his weight minutely to one side or the other, weaving through the trees like a shuttle through a loom. It was terrifying and exhilarating and Sally found herself whooping with him until she realized that wasn't going to help their attempts to hide.

"Shut up, Jet! We're hiding from the bad guys," she said, and then she began to giggle out of adrenaline and fear and the simple joy of being alive.

"Whoops," was all he replied. And then, "So where should we hide?"

"In our secret hideout, silly."

The hideout sounded much more impressive than it really was. It was just a hollowed out cave that ran under the branches of an oak. Strather's Creek ran alongside it, and over the years the trickling water had eaten away at the ground. Finally, the earth had given up the fight, and the result was a nice-sized sinkhole that you really couldn't see until you were right on top of it. Jet fell into it once, spraining his ankle in the process. After that, it became their secret lair—the place they staged all of their made up adventures of Jet Blackwood and Calamity Sue, or sometimes just a hideout from Eugene Falks and his buddies.

Chances were that the Steel Syndicate wouldn't know about the hideout because James had never figured out where it was. He could have ratted out a lot of things, but that wasn't one of them. Sally and Jet had sworn a pact never to reveal the location to anyone else, because what good was a secret hideout if you told everyone about it? None, of course.

As they got closer to the creek, Sally began to worry. This whole flight thing was kind of fun once you got used to it, but there was just one problem left to solve. They were going way too fast to land without both of them eating dirt.

"Slow down!" she yelled.

He thumbed the throttle. Nothing happened. He tried again and then looked at her with a stricken expression. "Sally, it's stuck!"

"Oh no," she moaned. First the original booster and now the trigger? This was what happened when you didn't properly test your inventions, and she'd never make that mistake again. The worst part was that she couldn't reach it, not without untying herself from the harness. She'd almost certainly fall. "What are we going to do?"

He took a long, thoughtful breath, surveying the landscape before them. "I've got an idea. Trust me!" he responded. And really, she had no other choice in the matter, so she did. It's not like she could demand that he stop the flying machine so she could get off. If she could, they wouldn't have had a problem in the first place.

He began to weave back and forth to cut down their speed a little as they neared their hiding spot, but as they approached it, they were still going pretty fast. Sally found herself rocketing straight toward the sturdy trunk of the oak. She'd known it was going to end this way.

"Hold on," he said.

One of Jet's hands released her waist, and she felt herself begin to slip from his remaining hand. Her worry about the tree was replaced by a very real fear that she was going to fall. She twisted, wrapping her arms more securely around his neck and hooking her ankles over his. The exhaust from the engine began to bake her socks, but it was a small price to pay for continuing to live.

He loosened his belt, pulling it from the trouser loops with a flourish. It came free moments before he twisted, heading up through the tangle of branches. Despite his best efforts, they were whipped and lashed by the tree. It seemed to Sally that more altitude was the last thing they wanted.

"Are you nuts?" she shrieked. But he just grinned in response.

Finally, Sally realized what he was doing. The air-cooled engine was designed to push the tractor along the ground. She'd made the air vents horizontal; flying straight up meant that no air would get to the engine, overheating it. The only question was how high they'd be when it happened. She waited breathlessly, trying to resist the urge to look down.

The engine sputtered, coughed, and then cut out completely as its engine locked due to lack of air flow. They began to fall back down, branches breaking underneath them with snaps and crackles. The impact slowed their descent, but it was still going to hurt when they reached the bottom. Jet kept trying to loop the belt over a branch as they fell, but that was harder than it looked. Their landing probably would have been extremely rough if the harness hadn't snagged on one of the thicker branches. They jerked to a stop, nearly tearing Jet's arms off and ripping her overalls a little as the straps tightened around them. She couldn't complain. They'd stopped about ten feet from the ground, and a little rope burn was much better than the alternative.

They hung there for only a moment before the branch gave way with a snap. Sally went flying down into the creek, rolling head over heels down the slope and into the water with a splash. The weight of the engine pulled Jet straight down into the exposed roots of the tree, which cracked under the weight. The landing wouldn't have been so bad if he hadn't landed flat on his back with the propulsion system underneath. His back arched as the metal dug into his ribcage. He let out a groan of pain.

"Jet!" Sally sat up, mucky water plastering her hair to her face and running in rivulets down the front of her shirt. "Jet, are you okay?"

He groaned again, and she scrambled up the slope to take a look at him. He lay on his back with his arms and legs flailing like a stuck turtle. She couldn't help but laugh.

"Sally," he said feebly, "I think I'm really hurt bad. It feels like something's stabbing me, and it hurts to breathe."

She sobered quickly. "Your ribs aren't broken, are they?"

He tested his ribcage with a finger, winced, and then shrugged. "They hurt like the dickens, that's all I know."

"Gimme a second, and I'll get you up."

A quick survey of the situation made it instantly clear that this was easier said than done. If he hadn't been injured, she could have just pulled him to standing, but with damaged ribs any twisting of the spine would hurt him badly. He was still attached to the harness, and the weight of the engine pulled on his injured torso. The straps were now badly tangled in the roots. She debated making a lever out of one of the larger branches that dotted the edges of the creek, but then she risked breaking more of the roots. No roots meant no hideout, and they needed a good hiding place more than ever now. Something told her that Jet wasn't going to be up to running for it after that fall.

The only thing left to do was to find some way to get the straps off him. She squelched her way up onto the tangle of roots, trying not to jostle him too much in the process. Dirty water dripped off her hair into his face. He closed his eyes and reflexively startled away from the droplets, hissing in pain.

"Sorry," she murmured. "Listen, this might hurt, but I've got to untangle you. Unless you have a pocket knife? I left mine in the workshop."

"Nope," he said, his lips white with pain. "Just get it done."

"I'm sorry," she said nonsensically, reaching around his body and fumbling along the straps. She wished she'd seen how he'd rigged the harness, but she'd been a little too distracted at the time to fully appreciate his design. Now she'd have to navigate it by feel while crouching over the injured body of her best friend on a somewhat unstable web of tree roots with the faint sounds of pursuit in the distance.

She cocked her head, her fingers stilling on the smooth weave of the straps. She could hear faint voices, lots of them. There was a chance that it was her brothers, or maybe some kids looking to set snares by the creek. But she was pretty sure it wasn't either of those things. They only had a few minutes to hide, and if they couldn't get under cover in time, they were probably goners.

The clasp had to be somewhere near the spine; she went for it, eliciting another hiss from Jet. Her fingers touched metal; she groped at the simple mechanism, following the curve of the strap as it doubled forward and then back upon itself, creating enough friction to hold it in place. It really was a smart design.

"I've got to give it to you," she said, beginning to inch the strap slowly through the maze-like binding, "I couldn't have woven this harness better myself."

He grinned, but sweat beaded on his upper lip, and his whole face had gone blotchy with pain despite her best efforts not to hurt him any more than he already was. His ribs were broken, all right. She refused to entertain the thought that it might be something even worse.

"Yeah? You should name it after me, then."

"The harness?" she said lightly. This was all going to be okay. She was going to get him out of here, and they'd hide, and he'd be fine, and later on she'd laugh at how frightened she'd been. It was a nice thought, but it didn't stop her hands from shaking. She knew he could feel it, but neither of them wanted to say it out loud. It was much easier to pretend confidence, to be strong for each other, even if that strength was a big fat lie. "That's not good enough for you, mister. No, I'm naming the engine after you."

"The Black engine?" he wrinkled his nose. "I'm not sure I like it. People will think you're talking about the color."

"No, silly. We'll call it the Jet engine."

This time, his smile was real. And when the strap finally came loose of its bindings, she managed to smile back.

It didn't take too long to maneuver Jet into the hideout, but it felt like an eternity. Any movement at all was clearly painful, and he was drenched in sweat by the time she got him tucked away in the corner. She wanted to bind his ribs, but she wasn't entirely sure that creek damp fabric was the best choice, and it was all she had. Plus, she still had so much to do.

She worked the jet engine out of its tangle of roots—a process that was much easier without Jet himself in the way—and rolled it into the hideout. Then she sprinkled a few handfuls of dried leaves and crabgrass over the damaged wood and used a branch to erase all traces of their passing on the ground. It wasn't perfect; any decent tracker would have spotted them from a mile off, but she was counting on the fact that these city slickers had no idea how to hunt down prey. With luck, they'd walk right on past.

For once, their luck held. No sooner did she drop into the hideout and carefully cover her tracks when she heard the sound of crunching footsteps, muffled curses, and breaking twigs. If the men had been hunters, they would have starved, because they were making enough noise to frighten off every animal in a five mile radius. As inept as they were, Sally had to admit she was quaking in her boots a little, and it would have been nice to cling to Jet for comfort except that she was too terrified to even twitch. They probably wouldn't hear her move. But probably wasn't good enough.

"I swear they went this way," said one gruff voice with "city" written all over it.

"Nah. I keep telling ya they're over there," answered another.

"This is stupid," added a third. "No way are we going to find them. The Don's lost his marbles."

"Ssssh!"

The sound came from right above them, accompanied by a shower of dirt. Jet jerked reflexively and then clamped his mouth shut on the groan of pain that tried to escape. There was a moment of heart-stopping silence. Had the men heard him?

"Don't say that, man," said the first man. His voice began to grow farther away. "He hears you say something like that, and you're a goner."

"Well, who's going to tell him?"

"Not me. But it's still a risk. He doesn't take criticism well."

Someone snorted. "Understatement."

The voices grew progressively fainter, and Sally began to relax. They hadn't noticed the hideout when they were right on top of it. All she and Jet had to do was hold out here for a while. They'd leave eventually, and then she could get some help. Maybe she'd drive Calamity down to the creek and cart him back on that. After all the work she'd done on the racing tractor, it was a smooth ride and wouldn't jostle him too badly. As far as plans went, it was a pretty good one.

Then she heard a familiar voice say, "Hey! You're looking for Sally Slick, aren't you?

She almost forgot the whole hiding bit and groaned. It was Eugene Falks, and he was using his suck up voice—the one he used to convince all the adults that he wasn't really pounding someone's face into the ground; it was just *playing*. Now she was scared. Of course neither she nor Jet had been stupid enough to tell him where the hideout was— half of the time they were hiding out from *him*—but he'd spent a lot of time out in the woods, and he might be able to find them even if the city slickers couldn't.

"You know where she is, kid?" The man's voice turned oily with promise. "I'll make it worth your while if you tell me."

"She and her runt friend have a hideout around here somewhere. I'm not sure exactly where, but it's close by. They run for the creek to hide whenever we come around. Me and my pals aren't to be trifled with, if you know what I mean."

Sally's heart sank. She'd always thought of him as a big dummy, but apparently Eugene was smarter than she'd given him credit for. She began to look wildly around for some way to escape, but even if she could manage to climb out of the hideout without anyone noticing, she couldn't leave Jet behind. And he was in no shape to climb anything.

"Sure, kid. Whatever you say. So she's probably somewhere's around here?"

"I'd go right off the water if I was her," said Eugene. "That way, if someone was trying to track me, I could make for the creek, and they wouldn't be able to follow my footsteps. I could come out anywhere along the edge without leaving a trail."

"You heard the kid," said a voice that sounded a lot like Frankie Ratchet. "Fan out. Look for hiding spots along the creek."

By this time, Sally had moved herself inch by inch back toward Jet. They were plastered against the back of the hollow, legs curled up against their bodies to make themselves as small as possible. She could tell from the stiff way that he held himself that Jet was hurting bad, but he didn't complain. He nestled his face in her hair, and she held on to his arm, and together, they waited for the end.

CHAPTER 22

Under many circumstances, Sally would have been very embarrassed to be cuddling with Jet. She wasn't the cuddling sort, after all, and even if she had been, Jet was her best pal. He wasn't the kind of boy that made all the girls bat their eyelashes and twirl their hair while they tried to catch his attention at the Harvest Celebration dance. Sally knew it happened—not because she was one of the hair-twirlers but because she was usually hanging around with the boys and talking about motors when the hair-twirlers attacked.

But as the voices got louder, and escape became more and more impossible, she found herself hugging him. Not too hard because of his ribs, but hugging him nonetheless. She'd gotten him into this mess, and he'd never complained. He'd come to her rescue more than once. It seemed like a real pity to have it all end here. He could have become something really spectacular. So could she.

"It'll be okay," she whispered into his hair, not quite sure if she was trying to reassure him or herself.

"I won't let them hurt you," he answered. At one time in their lives, she would have scoffed. She would have written it off as silly bravado from all those adventure books. But after everything that had happened, it made her feel better to know that, no matter what, they would still have each other's backs.

"I see them!" yelled Eugene. "Down here! Under the tree."

His long, horsey face appeared in a gap between the roots, and he grinned. "Heya, girls." Then he spit on them. The loogie landed with a wet splat on the leg of Sally's overalls. She wiped it off with the back of her hand and tried not to think of Ma finding her body on the ground and bemoaning the fact that her daughter wasn't even dressed like a lady when she died.

That thought made her teary, and the tears made her mad. When Frankie Ratchet grabbed her by the arm and pulled her out, she responded by clamping her hand into a fist and popping him one right in the nose. His head whipped back sharply; his eyes teared. Blood began streaming out of his right nostril. But his grip on her arm didn't loosen one bit, and he actually grinned at her.

"You've got spunk, missy. I like that. Reminds me of my girl."

"Is she a Syndicate bully, too?" Sally shot back.

Behind them, a pair of thugs dragged Jet out of the hideout. He tried in vain to keep his legs under him, but it was a futile effort. They slipped out from beneath him, eliciting another groan of pain.

"Stop, you monsters!" Sally yelled. "Mr. Ratchet, make them stop. His ribs are broken; they're hurting him."

"First you punch me, and now you're making demands?" But Frankie Ratchet sounded more amused than anything else. "Boys, be gentle with our captive here, will you? We don't want him damaged too badly when we present him to the Steel Don. You know how he gets."

They must have known all too well, because both men went completely white in the face and began to handle Jet like he was made of fine crystal. Ma had a set of crystal vases once. Then her brothers came along, and now it was down to one vase that she guarded like a mother lion with a very delicate cub.

"Thank you," said Sally.

"Yeah, thanks," Jet added weakly.

"Don't mention it." Frankie Ratchet pinched his nose to stop the bleeding, checked for blood on his fingers, and finally seemed happy with the result after two or three tries. Between the scarred face and the blood smeared across it, he looked quite dangerous indeed. But Sally felt better knowing he was there. He might be a crook, but he was a crook with honor, and that had to count for something. Actually, the more that she thought about it, he reminded her of someone. The way he kept calling her "missy." The faint undertones of an accent he'd clearly worked hard to obscure. It took her a moment to make the connection, but when she did, she couldn't believe it.

"Do you know the Creep?" she blurted, as he began to lead her away from the hideout.

His eyes narrowed and his hand tightened painfully on her bicep. "Hush, missy."

"Answer the question or I'll scream it."

After a long pause, he said, "He was my little brother." Past tense. Apparently, he knew about the Creep's death. Sally couldn't imagine working for someone who had ordered the murder of your own flesh and blood. Unless you were planning to topple the organization from the inside. Her heart leapt with renewed hope. "How do you know about him?" asked Frankie Ratchet.

"He's..." Sally trailed off, not entirely sure how to explain this without sounding like a complete fruitcake. But there was really no way to get it out without just going for it. "He's a ghost now. Doktor Proktor hit me with the Visionator—his ghost-seeing ray—and the Creep and I made a deal. I fixed the BEM robot body and gave it to him so he could save his wife and kids, and he agreed to help me in return."

Frankie Ratchet blinked, trying to process this very strange statement. He seemed about to say something, but then one of the other Syndicate men came up beside him and asked what they should do with Eugene Falks, and that was the end of that conversation.

"I deserve a big reward for leading you to her, don't I, sir?" asked Eugene, grinning. "I'll take cash if you got it."

"I don't like snitches," said Frankie Ratchet, glowering. "Got a convenient cow patch to throw him in, Miss Slick?"

Grinning, Sally gave them directions. She liked the idea of Eugene getting thrown head first into a stinking cow pie. For some reason, he didn't share her amusement. He thrashed and cursed and tried to break free without making any progress. Then he started spitting again until one of the thugs cuffed him on the ear. She almost felt sorry for him as they dragged him away. Almost, but not quite.

But the satisfaction didn't last long. Frankie Ratchet led the way to a motorcar waiting in the lane. Sally hoped for an escape opportunity; maybe she could slip away as soon as his back was turned. But he was too smart for her. He put Jet into the front seat of the car after her, and Jet couldn't move fast enough to make a break for the trees. She wouldn't have left him behind anyway, but it had been a nice thought.

The car started with a rumble and a lurch. Sally could think of about fifteen ways she could have made the ride smoother, but she wasn't going to offer to fix his suspension system. It seemed pretty fruitless since she was about to die. And she couldn't continue talking to Frankie Ratchet about the Creep, because the backseat was full of men in black suits. It was too bad, because she felt like maybe he'd help them if she could only talk him into it. She studied his profile: the hooked nose, the long, jagged scar that tweaked the corner of his mouth, and the set determination of his chin. Someone like Frankie Ratchet could stand up to the craziness of the Steel Don. It was just a matter of convincing him that it was worth the effort.

"I wonder what my *brothers* are doing now," she said, as idly as she could. "I'm just glad they're safe." Frankie didn't say anything, but his hands tightened on the steering wheel. She was determined to try again. "It would really bother me if they were in danger. I'd want some-body to do something. I'd really owe them after that."

Frankie Ratchet cleared his throat and proceeded to ignore every-thing she'd just said. "We'll be there in a minute. The Steel Don wants me to bring you two right to him."

"To make an example of us, right? He is aware that we're teenagers, right? He's going to hurt us, and you guys are acting like that's okay."

Jet clamped his arm tighter around his ribs and said softly, "You tell them, Sally."

"You can still do the right thing. Let us go before you get there, and no one will know you even found us in the first place. And if they hap-pen to capture us again, we won't tell. Pinky swear."

"I can't do that, missy. I'm honestly sorry it has to turn out this way."

"But your bro—"

"Enough!" His shout cut her off. "We're here."

She looked out the window, frowning. A bunch of motorcars choked the road in front of the mill, parked in such cockeyed disarray that it looked like the drivers had just rolled to a stop at random and decided to give up any attempt at organization. An oversized tractor sat in the middle with a long trailer attached to the back. A series of tarps tethered over the top obscured the contents from view. Under different circumstances, Sally would have tried to peek inside. As it was, she was too busy looking for something she could exploit, some opportunity that might save them. Maybe her brothers would realize she was gone? Maybe they'd get help. They'd rush out from under the tarp at any moment now, and James would be with them because he'd realized how wrong he'd been to abandon her, and then they'd free her and Jet, and...

As Frankie Ratchet led her from the car, she was still dreaming of rescue. He took her toward the door of the mill, and she kept her hopeful eyes on the cars. Nothing happened. He opened the mill door, letting out a puff of flour-scented air, and nudged her inside. The door closed behind her without any sign of her brothers.

Jet seemed to pick up on her growing despair despite the pain that had dampened his usual keen powers of observation. He tapped her on the shoulder. "You okay?"

"Aside from the part where we're about to be killed by a metal-faced madman? Sure."

He chuckled. "That'll never happen. It's not how Jet Blackwood and Calamity Sue's adventure is supposed to end. And it's *definitely* not how Jet Black and Sally Slick's adventure is supposed to end."

"How can you be so optimistic at a time like this?"

"How can you *not*? We've gotten out of worse scrapes before."

She might have agreed with him, but at that moment they emerged into the main room of the mill. One look at what was inside and she realized that she'd been all too right. They were in even more trouble than she'd imagined.

CHAPTER 23

The Steel Don stood in the middle of the mill, flanked by all the machinery. He dry washed his hands in overdone maniacal glee that made her want to roll her eyes. She would have too, if only he hadn't had that inhuman metal face. Someone who was willing to weld a mask to his noggin wasn't just *acting* insane. He was the real deal, and crazy people couldn't be anticipated. She had to keep reminding herself that Frankie Ratchet wouldn't be cowed by just anyone. If he considered the Steel Don a real threat, so should she.

But it wasn't the Steel Don that worried her. It wasn't the handful of about ten or fifteen of his flunkies scattered around the room. It wasn't even the occasionally visible handle of a gun sticking out from underneath their tailored suit jackets. It wasn't the still, silent mill machinery, or the vague fog of wheat particles in the air, or the small pile of flour bags off to the side, waiting to be transported out to the loading dock behind the building.

Standing near the windows was a phalanx of robots.

They weren't quite the same as the BEM she'd reconstructed. That model had been a little unbalanced, with wider hips than necessary in an attempt to keep the thing stable. As she'd been working on it, she'd already made vague mental plans to improve upon the design. Doktor Proktor must have come to the same conclusion, because these robots were similar, yet much more streamlined. She was willing to bet that this model was faster than the original BEM by a long shot.

"Meet BEM-2!" shouted the Steel Don gleefully. "They're the ideal enforcers—no conscience, no hesitance, and inhuman power at their disposal. Once everyone sees what these boys are capable of, no one will dare to oppose me. I'll rule Chicago with an iron fist. All other crime syndicates will bow to my rule!"

Sally began to look around the room. She knew this part of the adventure quite well. This was the part where the villain, flush with triumph, launched into a long and drawn out monologue about how he was awesome and the hero was stupid. Meanwhile, as the villain was congratulating himself on how brilliantly evil he was, the hero would work out a way to defeat him. This sounded like a bang up idea to her, especially the part where the villain was defeated, but how was she supposed to take out eight robots on her own? She didn't have the Creep's insight into their design like she'd had with BEM-1, and she was willing to bet that the innards were significantly altered from the version she'd seen. Even if she could figure out a weakness, it's not like she could take machinery apart with her bare hands. And even if she could do *that*, the guards would shoot her.

In short, the odds were pretty insurmountable, but she kept looking around anyway, trying to find a loophole she could exploit. This couldn't be the end. She refused to give up.

"I'm talking to you!" The Steel Don leaned into her face, spitting the words all over her cheek in his fury. "You had better listen when I'm talking to you! People who ignore me make me angry!"

"Sorry," she said, trying not to let on how scared she really was. "I was listening. You were saying how you were going to unite your Syndicate with...what? The European Meat Syndicate, was it?"

He blinked. "The what?"

"European Meat Syndicate. Isn't that what you said?"

"No, I..." He shook his head and then finally seemed to realize that she was poking fun at him. He glowered. "I will allow you your jokes, child. It is of no import. You'll serve your purpose regardless."

"And what purpose is that?" Now that she'd started mouthing off, she couldn't seem to stop herself. "Are we leading the robot parade through town? I think I have some ticker tape at my house. Want me to run and get it?"

"No." His mouth stretched in an inhuman, silver grin. "You will be the demonstration of the power of my robot army. The world will see what happens when I'm displeased."

"What's that? Do you get stomach problems? I'll make you a tonic."

Jet hissed, looking worriedly at the Steel Don, who was practically steaming by this point. And Frankie Ratchet seemed to be choking. His face was bright red, and he coughed and sputtered behind his cupped hand. One of the other mobsters pounded him on the back until the attack subsided. Everyone waited with stunned expressions to see what the Steel Don might do.

He didn't disappoint. He stomped over to Frankie Ratchet, muttering angrily under his breath the entire time, and grabbed the newly named jet engine. "I'll show you what happens to people who defy me." He pointed it at her like it was a gun and began to search for a handily labeled *on* button. Naturally, he didn't find one, because Sally never labeled her inventions. If you couldn't figure it out yourself, you weren't smart enough to use it. Luckily for her, the Steel Don fit into that category.

Unable to activate the jet engine, he decided to throw it at her instead. It bounced once and then skidded to a stop at her feet. She couldn't help herself. She let out a choked guffaw that echoed around the room. The whole thing was so stupid. It felt like one of Henry's pranks. At any moment, he was going to leap out and yell, "Fooled ya!"

But he didn't. Instead, the Steel Don pulled a familiar looking control device out of his suit pocket, pointed it at the robots, and yelled, "Rip her arms off!"

"No!" Jet yelled, lunging toward her despite the pain. One of the mobsters kicked him to the ground and then shoved a foot into the small of his back, pinning him there. Sally wasn't sure if she could really hear the grinding of his broken ribs or if she was imagining it, but either way it had to be agonizing. He screamed and went limp.

"Jet!" She wanted to run to him, but there was no way to get past the robots. They began to move toward her in precise unison, and just as she'd thought, this version was a lot quicker than the last model. After a moment of wide-eyed shock while her brain processed the fact that he'd really just ordered her dismemberment, she realized she ought to get out of Dodge. She turned around and ran straight into a thug, who shoved her back into the room hard enough to send her sprawling on the floor, skinning her knee.

She barely felt it. Her heart was pounding as the robots closed in on her, a silent silver semicircle of death. One of them leaned down toward her; its metal hand closed on her forearm. She struggled against it halfheartedly, knowing that there was no way her puny strength would ever prevail. She wondered if there would be much pain when her arms were ripped off, or if she'd pass out before the real hurt began. Part of her hoped for the latter. The other part cursed the first part for giving up. There was always a way out, even in the most dire of circumstances.

Her eyes lit upon the stacks of flour in the corner, and she instantly knew what to do.

CHAPTER 24

Sally Slick sprawled on the floor in the middle of a circle of robots intent upon pulling her arms off, one wrist already clamped in an unyielding metal grip. Her best friend had fallen into unconsciousness only a few feet away. There were men with guns clustered around the mill, as well as a crime lord with a metal face who practically capered with glee at the idea that he was about to witness a dismemberment. She was completely alone and without any hope of rescue, but still, her heart leaped with excitement.

She reached out with her one free hand, barely evading the searching grips of the BEMs, and thumbed the trigger to the jet engine, praying that it wasn't still stuck in place. But the fall must have dislodged it. The contraption roared to immediate life, torching one of the robots in the intense heat of its exhaust and blistering the skin on Sally's leg even though it wasn't directly in the line of fire. The metal man was blown over by the expelled air as the engine rocketed across the room.

The Steel Don barely managed to launch himself out of the way of the oncoming missile. He sprawled on the floor as the jet flew overhead, but Sally wasn't upset by that at all. He wasn't her intended target.

The jet hit the sacks of flour with a whomp and a whoosh, and the air turned white. As in the Golden Pagoda, Sally remembered to take in a big lungful of air before it became too thick to breathe. That much flour in the air could make a person choke. And what it could do to the exhaust system of a robot...

Assuming that this system was similar to BEM-1's, she was counting on the fact that gumming up the exhaust with flour would cause the BEM-2 to overheat. And she was counting on it working fast. It was her only possibility of escape, and it actually worked. It was too hard to see at first, what with the white clouds that filled the room, but she felt the robot's incessant tugging slow and finally stop altogether. She began to pry desperately at the fingers around her arm, forcing them open. The mechanical hand finally opened, and she stood up, lifting her shirt to her mouth to filter the air. She had to get Jet out of here before the Don regrouped.

She stood up, unnoticed in the circle of frozen, inoperable robots. She didn't see the Steel Don anywhere, but his men staggered about, coughing out white puffs of flour. Some made for the fresh air outside the doors. Jet still lay curled on his side a few feet away. She hurried to his side and covered his mouth with his pocket bandanna to filter the air, but she was too afraid to move him, what with the broken ribs and all. She couldn't pick him up on her own, and dragging him just seemed cruel. Maybe she could hide him and bring back help.

Someone grabbed her shoulder from behind, and she whirled around to punch at her captor. This time, Frankie Ratchet was ready. He caught her fist easily and deflected it off to one side.

"Easy," he said, his voice muffled by the handkerchief cupped over his mouth and nose. "I'm not here to hurt you. I'll carry your friend out."

Trusting him was stupid, but what other choice did she have? Hiding Jet wasn't much use if Frankie Ratchet knew where he was. So she nodded and kept a lookout while he hefted Jet up into his arms. Jet gave a little moan of pain, which made Sally feel incredibly relieved and hugely guilty at the same time. At least he was alive.

No one seemed to care as they made their way to the door. Probably the other men assumed that Frankie had them in custody. Maybe they were right. But either way, they made it out the door unharmed.

They emerged out into a semi-circle of flour-dusted men who coughed and sputtered out still more of the white stuff. Frankie Ratchet didn't pause. He led Sally toward one of the cars, opened the door, and put Jet inside. The boy curled up protectively over his left side but otherwise didn't respond.

"Hey!" one of the men called. Croaked, really. Sally was starting to think that spending time around her was very bad for the lungs. "What are you doing, Frankie?"

"The Don wants these kids moved until he can figure out what to do with them." The lie came out without a twitch. Frankie Ratchet glowered at his subordinate. "You got a problem with that, Joey Two-Fist?"

Sally knew she shouldn't beam at him, because prisoners don't do that, but she'd never had much luck hiding her feelings. No matter how hard she tried to pout, she couldn't hide her relief. One look at her face, and Joey knew there was something fishy going on here.

"I just want to verify this with the Don," he said. "No offense meant, Ratchet, none at all. But you know how he gets when things don't go right. I don't want *my* arms to get ripped off."

He chuckled, and when no one joined in, his eyes narrowed. Sally could tell from the way Frankie Ratchet's hand tightened on her shoulder that he was bracing for action, if only she knew what she was supposed to do to help. Should she attack? Was she supposed to run? She decided to hide in the car with Jet and lock the doors. Maybe she could hotwire it and drive off. And then Frankie Ratchet could leap into the car as it was speeding away, and they'd...go somewhere. Somewhere safe. It sounded like a terrific plan except for the blank spots, and she was determined not to worry about those.

She felt the ground rumble before she heard anything. Joey and the rest of the white-tinged Syndicate men began to look around nervously, their hands going to their hips and coming back up again with wicked looking pistols clutched in them. They waved the weapons around like the threat of violence might make the ground stand still. At first, Sally thought it was an earthquake. She'd been through one once—it had taken out yet another of Ma's prized pieces of heirloom crystal. Ma had cried over it.

But it wasn't an earthquake. Sally heard the angry low of a bull and knew exactly what was happening, and there was no time to waste. The cavalry had finally arrived.

"Get on top of the car!" she gasped, tugging at Frankie Ratchet's wrist. He looked at her with complete confusion, opening his mouth to say something, but there was no time for conversation if they didn't want to get trampled like a slowpoke in Pamplona. "Shut up and climb!"

She tore herself out from under his grip and clambered up onto the roof of the automobile, crouching down low. The Syndicate men looked at her like she was nuts. They were crouched down behind the scattered motorcars as if whatever was making the rumbling noise might start taking potshots at any moment. Frankie Ratchet climbed up onto the car just in time. She had one moment to worry about Jet— would he be protected enough by the car door?—and then the cattle turned the corner.

Now she could hear the whooping calls of her brothers, driving the animals toward the men intent on hurting their little sister. Their voices were angry and triumphant and the best thing she'd ever heard in her life. The bulls didn't feel the same way. They didn't like to be yelled at, and the lashing of the whips made them skittish, and now they were mad. One of the larger bulls hit the side of a car, tearing into the door with a screech of metal. Right about that time, the mobsters realized that crouching on the ground wasn't the smartest place to be, and they began to make for high ground, but it was already too late. As Sally watched, one of them got a bull's head to the seat of the pants and went flying. The bull kept on running, a flag of black wool dangling from one of its horns. The men scattered, running for safety.

Henry and Carl followed the bulls, and they didn't stop, taking them around the building on a continued sweep. A stampede like this wasn't going to stop until the bulls ran out of gas, so they couldn't just stop. But both of them grinned like idiots when they saw her. Sally couldn't help returning the expression, and her knees went a little weak with the knowledge that finally, she was safe. This could all be over now.

The feeling of relief lasted all of about two seconds. Then she felt a prickle at the back of her neck. Someone was behind her, and the Steel Don was still at large. Terror washed over her once again. It took all her willpower just to turn around.

It wasn't the Don. There was one Syndicate man crouched atop a long, black car, and as she turned around, she found him pointing a gun at her. Even from far away, the muzzle seemed huge. She'd gotten shot with a BB gun once when James was goofing off with it. It had hurt like the dickens. Something told her this was going to be worse.

Frankie Ratchet took a calm step in front of her, shielding her with his body.

"No shooting kids," he said. "But I don't have a problem shooting people who think it's okay to shoot kids."

In a flash, he had a gun in his hand too, and mutual destruction seemed inevitable. Sally didn't want Frankie Ratchet to die after all he'd done for her and Jet, but she didn't know how to help. If only she could manufacture clothing that would stop bullets. She made a mental note to try to figure that out later. Right now, she was more concerned about how to keep her and Frankie Ratchet from getting aerated. Maybe she could grab him and throw them both over the side of the car? It had worked for Lucky Blake in *Fabulous Adventures #7*, so it was worth a try. She was just scouting a good landing zone when she heard something new.

This was a steady, heavy thump, different from the constant rumble of the stampede. But it seemed to completely unnerve Joey Two-Fist. He crouched atop the car, looking around wildly to place the sound. It wasn't difficult. The Creep, in his BEM robot body, came stomping around the side of the building.

"Sorry I'm late," he said, his voice clipped and precise and somehow metallic sounding. But it was still unmistakably his. Frankie Ratchet's gun dropped to his side.

"Billy?" he said. "Is that really you?"

"Yup." The Creep swung one of his long, heavy arms, almost as an afterthought. It struck Joey right in the chest, throwing him off the car and into the gravel of the roadbed. He lay there motionless. Sally didn't feel particularly bad for him.

"She said..." Frankie Ratchet swallowed. "The little missy here said you were a robot now. I have to confess that I didn't really believe her."

The Creep let out a digitized laugh. "Well, you shoulda. She helped get me a body so I can make sure my girls are safe."

"Good." There was a long silence, and then Frankie Ratchet said, "Listen, Billy, I'm sorry I didn't listen to ya before."

"You better listen now. The Don is nutso. You don't stop him now, it'll be too late. And then this robot arm will be punching *you*."

"No need. I'm listening now, brother."

"Good." The robot's silver hand rose to its temple in a jerky salute. "You okay, missy? I'm gonna skedaddle and get home to my girls now."

"Yeah, I think we're good, thanks. You figured out how to talk."

He nodded slowly. "My mouth don't move, but yeah. There's some bits in here that I can move to make noise."

"Neat. If you need a tune up, you know where to find me."

"I'll remember that. Thanks."

"Thanks for coming back for me. You didn't have to do that."

"Yeah. I did." The robot gave them both a sketchy salute. "See ya."

The two of them watched as the Creep made his halting, jerky way down the road, pistons hissing and servomotors humming. Sally imagined him walking down the train tracks all day and all night until he got home. She imagined the chaos of him crossing the streets of Chicago, climbing the steps to his building, the fear and wonder of his family as they opened the door to find Daddy changed in ways they'd never imagined. But they'd be safe, and she'd helped to make that possible. She felt a huge wave of pride. This was what she'd been built for. It was like something clicked in her head, and she knew nothing would ever be the same.

"So that's it, then," she said, unable to contain a sigh that was half relief and half disappointment. It was going to be impossible to return to her normal life now. How could she sit and listen to Miss Cranston drone on about sums after all that she'd been through?

But Frankie Ratchet was shaking his head. "Sorry, kid. It's not over until the Steel Don is out of commission. I stood by while he took out my brother because I didn't think he'd really do it, and I was wrong. Now I'm not resting until he's down."

"Okay," she said. She couldn't argue with that statement one bit. She didn't think she could rest easy knowing that madman was out there either. "Let me just check on Jet, and we'll go hunt him down."

"That won't be necessary," said a voice from behind them.

CHAPTER 25

Sally and Frankie whirled around in unison to see Doktor Proktor standing next to the mill doors. His lanky frame was once again clothed in a stained white lab coat, but all traces of the doddering, absent-minded professor were gone. This man looked at them with a fierce intelligence behind the thick glasses, and for the first time, Sally could see him as the genius behind all of the fabulous inventions. Had his strange demeanor been an act all along?

James stood at his side, and her eyes went immediately to him. He was different somehow. He still had that proud tilt to his chin; his hair was still the same sandy brown, still cut short and proper. He still had the chip in his front tooth from the time he fell off the hay loft. But when he looked at her, there was none of the recognition that he'd once had, none of the brotherly protectiveness. He looked at her with cold appraisal like she was a stranger.

"James?" she asked tentatively. If Proktor had brainwashed her brother, she was going to make him pay.

"Sally." He nodded coldly. "I see you didn't die."

Forget wanting to save him. She decided to punch him instead. Only Frankie Ratchet's restraining hand on her shoulder kept her from doing it right then.

"Stay here," he murmured. "He's baiting you."

So she stayed there atop the car, fuming. After a moment, Doktor Proktor cleared his throat, looking vaguely disappointed. Maybe he'd counted on her rushing over. Then he could have grabbed her and left. She had to remember to keep her temper; Frankie Ratchet wouldn't be around to protect her forever. But it was easier said than done, especially after seeing how James had changed.

"Have you thought any more about my offer of employment, Sally?" The Doktor's weird accent was gone too. Now his voice was cultured, British, urbane. She couldn't figure out which voice was real and didn't much care.

"No way," she said automatically.

"You've seen what I'm capable of. And the BEM prototypes you've seen to date are already outdated. Take a look at this."

He gestured expansively toward the side of the building, and out came a machine that Sally couldn't have even dreamed of. This design took every disadvantage of the first two BEM models, streamlined it, and made it perfect. It was light and balanced and moved forward with the grace of a hundred acrobats. Its metal face swiveled to look at her, and the glowing orange of its eyes emitted a keen intelligence. She could almost feel it evaluating her.

In its arms, the Steel Don struggled.

"Put me down! I command you to have this machine release me, Proktor! We had a deal!" he yelled.

"Shut him up, Three," Proktor said, almost dismissively.

He didn't even have a control device, but the machine responded to his command anyway. The robot tucked the portly figure of the Don under one metal arm without any effort at all and clamped a metal hand over his metal face with a clang.

"Three?" asked Sally, trying desperately to resist the urge to climb off the car and take a look for herself. "This is the BEM-3?"

"I only made one," said Proktor. "The only way you'll see how I did it is by coming with me. As you can see, I no longer work for the Syndicate."

"You should come, Sally," James added, but his voice was hollow, like there was nothing inside of him anymore. It made her want to cry.

She shook her head. "I can't. It wouldn't be right. I can't leave my family, and I won't."

The Doktor hissed in disappointment. "Well then, I suppose we should be going. But the offer stands, my dear. You and I will be crossing paths many a time in the future. All you need do is hold out a hand to me, and I shall take it. Together, we could do many amazing things."

She wanted to shake her head and laugh at him for making such a ridiculous claim, but for some strange reason, she believed what he was saying. A man who could make a machine to detect ghosts could make one to see the future, couldn't he?

"I'll think about it," she said cautiously, but inside, she vowed that she'd do no such thing.

"I shall leave you with a parting gift, then. As a gesture of good faith." He nodded to Three, and for one heart-leaping moment, Sally thought she might get a good look at the robot after all, but it simply threw the Steel Don down at her feet instead. Frankie Ratchet was on him in a flash, taking away his weapons and placing a foot on the back of his former boss' neck while the metal faced man struggled on the ground beneath him.

But Sally stayed motionless atop the car, staring at her brother and willing him silently to come back home where he belonged. James didn't even seem to notice.

"We shall bid you adieu, then," said the Doktor.

"James, don't go!" she blurted. "Please! We miss you."

"You miss someone who no longer exists, Sally." Her brother spit the words at her, the emptiness in his eyes instantly replaced with howling fury. "I've seen what you'll become, and I refuse to live always in your shadow. *I'm* the eldest! I should be the one they all look up to! You took my rightful place!"

She shrank back before his red-faced, fist-clenched onslaught. "I didn't take anything."

"But you will, my girl," the Doktor sounded strangely satisfied by that. "You will. And I shall be waiting there."

"That's silly," she began, and she would have continued on, except that the Doktor waved his hand, and she could see a shimmering arc in the air where his hand passed. Something hung there—numbers and letters written in smoke—but before she could read them, they were gone.

So were Doktor Proktor, Three, and her brother.

After Sally'd had herself a good cry, the sheriff came and arrested a bunch of the Syndicate men, including the Steel Don. She'd begged Frankie Ratchet to stay and provide some evidence, but he'd refused.

"You think I'm a good guy, missy, but I'm not." He ruffled her hair fondly as he spoke. "Now, if you need anything, I'll come, because I admire your spunk. But I'm not about to go clean over some kid. Crime is in my blood, and sticking with blood is important. You understand."

"I guess," she'd replied. And maybe she *had* understood, but she hadn't liked it.

Jet finally woke up, extra sore from his rest in the car. His pa heard about what had happened and showed up with Doc Wilson to get him bandaged up. She'd never seen Mr. Black so proud of his son before.

He looked like he was ready to explode, and Jet's face was blazing red from embarrassment after the fifth time his dad stopped someone to tell them about "his son the hero."

Her brothers were scouring the township, trying to figure out where Mr. Lamont's prize bull had gotten off to. At some point after they'd borrowed his herd, it had wandered off, and the old farmer couldn't decide if he was angry at them or proud that his cattle had been the ones to subdue all the wanted criminals. All in all, it was the most excitement their sleepy little town had seen in ages, and Sally figured the boys would get off easy.

As for her, she sat alone with her back propped up against the side of the mill, trying to figure out how she felt about all of this. She wanted to go to bed, and to cry, and to run around and whoop with excitement all at the same time. It felt like the entire world had taken a big step to the left while she wasn't looking, and now everything was exactly the same but completely different all at the same time. She didn't know what to do now.

The crunch of footsteps in the gravel announced Ma's approach. She had Ralphie on her hip, and the baby cooed and smiled as he saw his sister. She gave a hesitant, shaky smile back.

"Hey, Ma," she said. "How's he doing?"

"Much better," Ma replied, settling down on the ground next to her daughter. "The cough's almost completely gone. Want to hold him?"

Sally hesitated and then took the blanket wrapped figure in her arms. He wrapped one hand around a lock of her hair and closed his eyes, immediately contented. She couldn't help but wonder—was this a sign that her adventures were over? Was the universe telling her that from here on out, it would be time to settle down and learn how to keep house and tend babies like a proper young woman? She felt torn in a hundred different directions.

"You know," said Ma, "the house we live in? Grandpappy didn't build it the way everybody says."

Sally blinked. "Huh?"

"I said that Grandpappy didn't build the house. Mostly, he carried the heavy things. Grandmama did it all. Designed it, and built the thing from the ground up. And when the general store couldn't get the stove model she wanted, she built her own. Took all the iron bits down to the blacksmith and made that man work night and day until he got the pieces just the way she wanted them."

Ma shook her head, chuckling at the memory.

"How come I didn't know this before?" asked Sally. She couldn't reconcile the tiny, wiry old woman she remembered from long ago with this new information, not at all. Her grandparents had died when she was young, but she thought she would have remembered this if she'd ever heard it.

"I think Grandmama didn't want a fuss. Pappy wouldn't have cared; he was proud that his wife was so talented. But so many people don't feel that way, and she was sensitive to that."

"So what are you saying? I should hide my skills like Grandmama did?"

Sally hung her head, trying not to feel ashamed. It wasn't her fault that she was built for adventure, was it? She couldn't help but feel that it was. Ma was ashamed of her, and that was the most horrible thing she could imagine.

"Not at all! Be proud! This is in your blood, and I for one am proud to see my mama in you."

"But that's not what proper young women do. I shouldn't run around in overalls and whack things with wrenches."

"If you hadn't, think about what would have happened," Ma said reasonably. "At the end of the day, I'm happy someone did something to stop those men. I don't care if that someone was a girl, only that they had guts and smarts enough to do it."

"So...it's okay with you? I mean, if I didn't want to stay here and farm and raise babies when I grow up?"

"Darling, you have time enough to figure out what kind of woman you're going to be. Whatever that is, I'll be proud. And I'm proud of my girl now, because she's a hero to me."

Sally felt her eyes prickle with tears, and for once, she didn't hold them in because she was afraid people would think she was weak. Maybe, just maybe, she could have it all. James had gotten so desperate to prove himself that it drove him to do terrible things, and look where it had gotten him. Now he was under the spell of Doktor Proktor, and she was certain that the scientist was only using him. And Eugene? He was so eager to prove that he was better than a mere girl, and it got him planted face first in cow dung.

That didn't mean she couldn't dream and work toward better things, not at all. But she was done with taking what she had for granted. She had the best family and friends anyone could ask for. Maybe she could use her love for them to drive herself to do more. Maybe it was okay to be a gushy, mushy girl sometimes, because when the chips were down, those feelings gave her things to fight for.

In her arms, her baby brother shifted, coughed once, and nestled into her. And Sally Slick smiled, imagining the new cradle she was going to invent for him. It would have a breathing apparatus, and an air filter, and an automatic rocker, and...

SALLY AND JET WILL RETURN IN...

SALLY SLICK
AND THE MINIATURE MENACE

COMING IN 2014

EVIL HAT
PRODUCTIONS

ABOUT THE PUBLISHER

Evil Hat Productions believes that passion makes the best stuff—from games to novels and more. It's our passion that's made Evil Hat what it is today: an award-winning publisher of games and, now, fiction. We aim to give you the best of experiences—full of laughter, story-telling, and memorable moments—whether you're sitting down with a good book, rolling some dice, or playing a card.

We started, simply, as gamers, running games at small conventions under the Evil Hat banner, making face to face connections with some of the same people who've worked on these products. Player to player, gamer to gamer, we've passed our passion along to the gaming community that has already given us so many years of lasting entertainment.

Today, we are turning that passion into fiction based on the games we love. And, much like the games we make and play, we need and *want* you to be part of that process.

That's the Evil Hat mission, and we're happy to have you along on it.

You can find out more about us and the stuff we make at *www.evilhat.com*.

ABOUT THE AUTHOR

Carrie Harris is the author of BAD TASTE IN BOYS and BAD HAIR DAY. Her husband is a ninja doctor, and her three kids are already in training to fight evil someday. She collects monster-themed clothing, is physically incapable of being serious for more than five minutes at a time, and dreams of racing a tractor someday.